Vanilla Smoke

Alena Daaé

Table of Contents

"Vanilla Smoke"

Puffs of sweet, steamy clouds—
inhale—
air floods his lungs
scent seizes my mind—
exhale—
smoke rolls off his tongue
and vanilla lingers
on his lips
that coil up
to a satisfied
smile—
sweet—
smoke—
sleep.

- *Nura Hart*

Chapter 1: Mint Gum

Gum smacks
between his teeth
mint slides
around his mouth—
on my tongue
sweet ice
dark, happy
James-Franco-smile
deep, throaty laughter
rippling in deep,
cold ocean depths
in his eyes that intoxicate
me with
one
cool
look.

- *Nura Hart*

I knew he was dangerous. My senses heightened when I met him, alert, but also utterly fascinated. Curiosity killed the cat, almost quite literally in my case. Like the wet, permanent marker smelling cat cadaver I dissected in high school biology. My cat had been pregnant—a little purple alien curled up in its dead, underdeveloped skin—never fully alive.

Cool mint shivers from the buds of my tongue to the goosebumps on my arms. The hot, salty wind of the summer night whistles around me as if my breath could provide cool, aloe relief to sunburns from the San Diego sun. Now it's the end of August, and my burns are cooling on their own.

He used to cool me—when his lips and tongue tasted mine. His breath, a relief of cold heroin that streamed and sedated my boiling veins. Maybe that's what kept me going back to him. And maybe that's because he's an addict himself.

"Don't fall in love with an addict," all the oh-so-wise ones say. But what they fail to tell you is that you also shouldn't let an addict say "I love you." Because *that's* when shit gallops onto the path of FUCKING TROUBLE congested with signs that warn you, in red:

TURN BACK

DO NOT ENTER

BEWARE OF HEARTBREAK

And you, you will idiotically ignore those signs like the stupid white chick in a horror movie. I'm that idiot. Goddammit. I kick a rock.

"OW! Shhi—" My toe throbs and screams at my mind's self-inflicted pain. *Idiot idiot idiot.*

I flop onto the sand and lay on my back, not giving a single goddamn *damn* that the sand will somehow crawl into my ass crack and boobs. So I roll around like it's snow.

"Well that's something you don't see every day."

I flip onto my back and poke my head up. I roll my eyes.

"Heyyy V," I huff.

She grins, then plops right next to me and tucks her blonde waves behind her ears. "Looks like you could use some *sane* company, Nura."

I sigh; I know she's here because I've spending a lot of time alone, but that's usually how I deal with things. I dwell in my misery for a while, then, when I'm ready, I splurge in some fun. You know, like go to a party and flirt with a cute guy or go to the movies on a rainy day. Though I don't party so much anymore.

I've been miserable this whole week and have dodged all calls and texts—that kind of misery tends to concern best friends. Vanessa is one of those friends.

"Well, I'm not so fun right now, so." I smack my gum and fold my arms across my chest, kind of hoping she'd leave so I can relish in blackness and not contaminate her. But I guess this is one of those times I probably need to be bothered. I've been alone too long—it's not healthy.

"That's okay. We can just chill. Dan's out with his friends for his twenty-second birthday anyway," she says, standing her ground. "You got any more of that gum? It smells *so* good."

I chuckle because I picture Dan, her boyfriend, dancing with his bush of brown hair flopping up 'n' down to the music in a club. I liked Dan, but I didn't get to spend as much time with V now. Maybe that's why I held onto Max so much.

I sit up and pull out a piece of gum from my pocket, the silvery blue wrapper shimmering in the moonlight.

Him. Everything seemed to remind me of him.

Max leaned over from the driver's seat and kissed me; his tongue slipped in my mouth, and his lips spread to a grin. "Mmmm, you taste good."

I bit my smiling, bottom lip. "Mint gum."

"You got anymore?"

I reached down by my feet for my purse and slipped him a piece of gum wrapped in silvery blue paper. He smiled and took it. "Thanks babe."

He hopped out of his car. I followed.

The bright beams of late June sunlight blinded me until we got inside his beach house. We'd only been seeing each other for a month at that point, but I'd gotten comfortable and familiar pretty fast, so whenever we went inside his house, I automatically turned left into the garage, which he had turned into a room for himself.

He blocked off his space with soft, long blankets that fell from the ceiling like a grey waterfall. Whenever I went through that waterfall, I was showered with beats of SoundCloud rappers pounding from the speakers. Whenever I went through that waterfall, I was showered with Max.

Literally, too. He's a whole six-feet and four inches and towered over me like a shower head. Neither of us really realized it, I think, except for when he had to hunch over to hug me. The atmosphere of our minds and auras just seemed like we fit so well, like sand and water. Warm and cold.

Loving and destructive.

Chapter 2: Sand and Water

Tryin' to find my wave my grind when she appears—

- MAX.

He swung the heavy, white door open.

"Hey," Nura smiled, shoulders hunched in her drapey white sweater.

"Hey," Max said, "Come in." He motioned her inside his beach house and went to the right to hop up the narrow, wood staircase. He looked back at the girl, the girl he'd only seen once just a few nights ago at the bar. Since then, he'd only seen pictures on her Instagram. She was beautiful in the pictures.

And she was beautiful now. Wavy dark hair with streaks of highlighted brown from the combination of sun and saltwater.

Soft, tan skin with a golden glow that he wanted to reach out for and touch.

He swayed up the stairs and looked behind him—stairs. *Where'd she go?* He peeked over the staircase. Nothing, no one, except him.

He shrugged. Maybe he was mixing memories again.

He walked into the kitchen and opened the fridge. Wrinkly fruit. Day-old pizza. Yogurt. The two end pieces of a loaf of bread that no one ever ate. Then he opened the freezer and grabbed a clear bottle on the side shelf. Vodka. He took a swig, then saw Nura leaning over the white tile counter, looking around the house as if ingraining every detail in her mind. *How long had she been standing there?*

"Want some?" he offered the bottle to her.

She scrunched her lips to the side and shook her head. "I'm good."

She walked over to the narrow, rectangle windows just above the round table in the small dining area and smiled. The sunlight beams revealed a golden tint in her brown eyes.

"Nice view, huh?" he said, stumbling around the counter to stand next to her. "Just a little view of the ocean right there." He pointed to the square of blue between two other identical houses in the gated neighborhood. The small view of his true home.

They talked for a little. He led her around the house, not much to show but lots to show at the same time. The guitar that he couldn't play as well as his brother. The long, blank mural he wanted to paint.
The little balcony with a table, six chairs, and a folded umbrella for when the sun was too bright.

She appreciated every bit of it— she listened. Didn't talk too much but she responded the way he wanted her to—impressed, her cheeks shining with her smile, eyes already lured toward him. From the moment he met her, this was how it was and would continue to be.

Colors gorged the scene—yellow and black and red—lemon bursts and pops of cherries in darkness. Light and blood, dim lamp light and dark hole of virginity given. Black and grey and white mix of night.

He fell onto his bed of grey sheets. Liquid buzzed through him. He reached his hand out, tapping on empty spaces like drums. He turned his head slightly.

Her body lay far, but he could touch her arm. Soft. Tan. Sleeping. She hadn't left him in the middle of the night. He turned and scooted his body over. Warmth radiated from her. He wrapped his arm around her and pulled her in until the arc of her back fit into him. She stirred, and a giggle rose from her chest—like the rays of sun that beat against him while he surfed in the cold ocean. Light, like her name. Her name meant light, apparently, though he didn't remember how he'd come to know that.

It was nice to wake up in the morning with a little gift next to him. Sweet and refreshing after a stir of drugs and alcohol. And that sunlight morning sex—*man*. A sweet, clean girl—fresh, minty breath, and hair billowed with soft, fruity perfume. He wanted to kiss her and kiss her again and again until his lips melted into her skin, right now.

Now.

In faint, yellow light.

He fell onto his bed of grey sheets. Liquid buzzed through him. He reached his hand out, tapping on empty spaces like drums.

Then he turned his head slightly:

A lifeless puddle of sheets.

He reached for his phone on the grey-carpeted floor next to his bed and scrolled through his phone history. He *did* call her last night. But she never answered—she never came over. Are *they* over?

What time is it anyway?

The bright numbers screamed: 7:00am. He still had some hours before work. He threw the phone back on the ground, then rolled over on his stomach, falling into blackness and dreams of her, of sand pulling into the waves and the waves crashing onto the sand—kissing and destroying.

Chapter 3: Black blood

A pool of bodies and red solo cups swirled around me in a pleasant, watery haze. The first semester of my sophomore year of college at UCSD, Labor Day weekend—one of the biggest party weekends for last-summer-hoorahs. My friends and I had come together, but at some point in the night, we'd forked in different directions. I stumbled my way to the dance floor.

The music thumped against my chest in the claustrophobic nightmare. I couldn't move through the crowd without accidentally brushing someone's ass. But I was too drunk to care, and that buzz moved my hips—'round and 'round.

A hand wrapped around my waist. I pressed the calloused hand against the sweaty skin of my belly and grinded against him, my head too fuzzy to care to wonder who it was. I smiled and shook my hair and gazed at the flicker of poison neon circles—the only source of light in the darkness.

"*OOOOH*!" A crowd of people shouted from the kitchen, probably around the beer pong table.

The hands on me turned my body around and pulled me away from the ocean of limbs.

"Whaterereya, wherya gonin'?"

"Don' worry—just need a little air," a smooth, velvety voice spoke in my ear, at least, I think that's what he said. Maybe he said I needed a little care. His arms, a cascade of muscle, dragged me forward. Blurs of faces and colors floated all around until a black shadow cloaked us.

Click.

A door swung open. Coldness swept over me as we entered the pitch-dark room, not even a window of blue night open.

Hell.

A heavy force pushed me forward, tossing me onto a bed that wasn't mine. The whip of air slapped me into somewhat clearer consciousness. Enough to question what was happening, at least. "Wa—wha—wa—"

"*Shhhhhh.*" A long, calloused finger pressed against my lips. I flicked it away, my whole body moving with my hand so I lay on my side.

"No, I—Ineedagohome," I whined, then forced myself to sit up. But before I could lift myself off the bed, his arms smacked me back down and his body weighed—sweaty and heavy—against mine.

"*Shhhhh.*" His hand stroked my hair. Soft, silent. Chills rolled down my spine.

"St—st—don't. *Stop*—" I rolled over, crawling toward the edge of the bed so that maybe the fall off the bed would sober me up enough to run. I knew I had to run. *Run*.

"Hey, don't fall there." He pinned me down, his hands like tight chains around my wrists. Fear rushed to my head, begging my body to sober up and fight and run. Fucking *run*! Do *something*!

"*He—Hel—help*!" I tried to scream, but my voice was too heavy to carry, and so it came out as if muffled by cotton. "*Some—some—hum, please*."

I took advantage of my free hand and tried to swing at the shadow above me, but he just wrapped his hand around it, as if I had simply lifted my arm in the air, then set it back down on the bed.

"*Help,*" I croaked.

"*Shhhhhhh*, it's okay." His whisper penetrated my ears, the cold poison paralyzing me. One hand fell onto my breasts, unwelcomed. Trailed under my skirt, unwelcomed.

Zzziiip. His bare legs pressed against mine. I squirmed under the body that contained my resistance with ease. Hyperventilation choked me while I struggled to get him off me. The air stuffed me; sharp aches pounded against my skull. I could barely move right. *Move. MOVE* DAMMIT *MOVE! DAMMIT!*

Why did I drink so much?

He shoved his hand in me and ripped my lace underwear down my legs.

"No . . ." I cried, sobs clutching my chest.

STOP! GET OUT! RUN NURA FUCKING *FIGHT!* But he pinned my body down, taking advantage of the many alcohols streaming through me, slowing every bit of me. I didn't want to die. But I wanted to die because I didn't want to deal with the aftermath.

And when he pushed inside me, breaking the unbroken. . .

I prayed for a peaceful death.

Rust poured
from my lips
red and torn
black hollow
broken, taken
"You *consented*"
yet I lament.

- *Nura Hart*

Chapter 4: Strawberry Milk Sex

the flavor of that smoke
that lingers on his tongue
as he tastes mine

puckers his lips
for one more kiss
then another
and another

until we're tangled in each other
and connected—
strawberry milk
sweet
creamy
cloudy

- *Nura Hart*

Two pink double lines appeared on the white stick.

Fuck.

I sit on the toilet of my bedroom bathroom in the apartment V and I will share. She hasn't moved in just yet. I thought about asking V to come with me and buy the test, but I don't want to tell anyone just yet. And although no one is here, I still lock the door, as if my parents are still around and might barge in.

Sometimes I wish they would.

My mother and father are dead. My father drank. My mother was in the car with him. He drove into a one-way street and that was it. I was eighteen and just started college. V was there for me, at least. I pretty much haven't had anyone expect V for the last few years.

And I wish I had the confidence that Max was that type of person—the type to be there.

I know I have to tell him either way. He called me last night, but I was asleep. We haven't talked for a week, but it feels like forever. Only a week apart, and already I have to go back to him. Will I ever get over him?

I look at the bathtub, and suddenly a hot, bubble bath sounds like the cure to all my headaches. So I turn the knob and wait for the tub to fill. Steam puffs up in clouds from the tub faucet as I pour the bubble soap. I strip down and turn off the water once it's filled, then dip my toes in.

The hotness smooths over my tense muscles as I slide inside the water. I lay down. The pink bubbles float with a strawberry scent. I touch my belly. There's a baby in there. His.

And yet again, I cannot escape him.

It was just three weeks ago that he told me he loved me.

DA DA DUN, DA DA DA DA DA DA DUN DA DA

"Should I Stay or Should I Go" by the Clash blared from my phone. My ringtone. The blue light glared in my eyes. I groaned in the darkness and emerged from sleep to check who was calling.

Max.

We were still together then, and so I always left my ringer on in case he called, even if it was past midnight. "Hello?"

"Heyy. What're you doin'?"

"Mmm. . .nothing, really." *Well, I was sleeping because I was waiting for you to call all night.*

But I didn't tell him that. I was just happy that he had called at all. My earlier disappointment evaporated.

"Yeah soo. . . like I don't think we should do this anymore, you know. . .not feelin' it," he said.

I froze. Ice-cold disappointment drenched me all over again. I knew he liked to tease me, but I was always afraid that one day it wouldn't be a joke. One day, he'd actually be tired of me.

I wouldn't let him know that though.

"Oh, okay. Cool. Guess I'll just . . .go now." I tested, waiting a bit before hanging up. He laughed.

"So are you coming over?"

"I thought you were breaking up with me?"

"What? Nooo, I'm kiddinnnnn'. I could never, like, do tha' to you, you're like the sweetest, most. . . gen—genuine, like, golden girl." My heart leaped and warmed like his words would make me a gold sun. "Come over babe. I mean, if you want. If it's not too inconvenient."

I sighed. I wanted to go over. I'd been waiting to go over and see him. He always kept me waiting, like a puppy by the door. But like the puppy, once I saw him, I was hopping and happy all over again. And I waited for those moments.

I was familiar with the road at night by then. It was a long stretch of green lights because either people were sleeping or too drunk to drive, and the soft beat of music thumping in the car made it a good reflective time.

I glanced at the rearview mirror, and though I didn't feel tired because of the Max-high I got whenever I was about to see him, the slight bags under my eyes told me otherwise. Something squeezed my heart. I would get this feeling often because of Max: the sensation of happiness despite the suffocation and stress. But there was a reason for it.

DA DA DUN, DA DA DA DA DA DA DUN DA DA

I pressed the green button on my phone as soon as I could.

"Hey," I said.

"Heyy can ya get me some fooood?"

"Yeah, sure, where at?"

Shuffling. Pause. More shuffling. "Uhm. . . In n Out's closed, so. . .Jack in the Box. It's like, the one by my house, you know what I'm talkin' 'bout? It's right by the sushi place we went to before."

"Yeah, I do. What do you want?"

I hit the first red light of the night, and the static in the phone call murmured black silence.

"Uhhh, just call me when you get there."

"Okay. Be there soon." A green light shone. I stepped on the gas.

"Thanks babe, Iloveyou" I almost stomped on the brake. A bang of silence slammed me. But then he caught himself and laughed. "Wait—uh, ha—I mean, I really really like you, ya know—"

My eyes grew wide and my heart exploded into—what? Fear? Excitement? A firework mixture of both? I let out a breath that sounded like a strained chuckle. "Uh, yeah yeah. I know. I'll call you when I get there."

"'Kay, love you," he said, *again*. I hung up and kept driving. *He loves me.* The road no longer stretched straight—it swirled and popped with hot pink and yellow from my wild heart. *Love you*. But another voice stabbed the bubbles of hope in me.

Don't get your hopes up, Nura. He's just drunk. Really drunk.

But was it hope I felt? Or confusion? I couldn't tell if I was happy or afraid or both.

All of the above.

I got to Jack in the Box and called him for his order. He asked for some chicken sandwich, curly fries, and a large Sprite. And when I told him I was on my way, he did it again.

"Love you."

He loves me.

I drove fast to his house, excited when he kissed me.

Then he ate. Offered me food. I shook my head. And we didn't talk about the L word like I had hoped we would. And I didn't say it back. But he kissed me again, said, "Thank you," and joked around again saying I should go home.

I almost did, but he pulled me onto the bed with him and he fell asleep. But I could not think about anything except those words that actually came from his lips, in his deep, smoky, cool voice, until I finally closed my eyes, knowing, hoping that I would wake up to those words again.

The next morning, with the sunshine streaming from the cracks of the garage door, the "I love yous," from the night seemed to express itself in his touch. He was gentler than usual. He pulled my body close against his, so our bodies brushed against each other and bathed in warmth.

He did what he thought would please me, and he did. Kissed me everywhere, slowly, rhythmically, musically—like he was writing a song on my body. When he pressed into me as soft as milky silk, he clouded my head with sweet strawberries in his breath. He comforted me with his body, smooth and ridged with curvy muscle, against mine.

It was the closest thing I had ever felt to *really* "making love." Every other time had been good enough to heal my first time away from my memory, like a sheet of ointment on a cut. But I had never expected to find the wound almost healed when I decided to have sex with Max.

When he came, he brushed a towel over me, cleaned himself, then grabbed out his vape. I watched the smoke dissipate as it flowed from his lips. I breathed it in next to him—it smelled like soft, sweet strawberries, and something else I couldn't place that made it so smooth in my lungs.

"What's that flavor?" I asked.

He took another hit. "Strawberry milk."

I wrapped my arms around his and traced the rose tattoo on his shoulder with my finger.

"Do you remember last night?" I asked.

He blew out smoke. "Yeah."

"Hmmm."

"Why?"

I shook my head. "No, nothing. Just curious."

I wanted to ask him if he meant it. But I didn't. I was afraid of getting an answer I didn't want. I could've left, but what he didn't know was that I *couldn't* leave. I *wouldn't* unless he told me to leave, maybe not even then. I loved him. Even if his "I love yous" were a result of the alcohol, alcohol was a truth serum. Even if he didn't remember saying so, I would.

I would remember everything.

Though I knew I could not change him, I decided that I would be there no matter what—I would be there whether he changed or didn't. I would be there until the day came when I couldn't be there anymore due a serious lover or perhaps too many empty promises. I would be there for as long as I could hold on to those strawberry milk moments.

But what if I didn't want to hold on anymore?

Chapter 5: Truth Serum

Smokin' blunts and can't get enough—

- MAX.

The stretch of road rolled in front of him as he rode on his skateboard, surprisingly balanced for how much alcohol he drank that night.

He was even able to hold the phone to his ear and call the girl from the bar. Nura, her name was. Nura. She had left with a friend of hers, some tall blonde.

And he left not too much later—or maybe it was a lot later, he couldn't tell. But she was still scalded in his mind: her curves, her smile, the dim, bar lights sparkling in her eyes. She seemed familiar somehow.

"Have I seen you before?" He asked. She laughed and shrugged.

"If you've been to UCSD party, then maybe," she said. He was twenty-three and had never really finished college. He still went to parties to see some of his friends that did go there, but he would've remembered her—he would've tried to talk to her then.

It didn't matter either way, 'cause he knew her now. He called her that same night, buzzed—okay, maybe a little more than buzzed.

"Hello?" she answered in a small yet charmed voice.

"Heyyy, it's Max."

She giggled. Bubbles floated up his chest at the sound. "Hey, what's up?"

"What're ya doin'?"

She let out another giggle and he was high as the bubbles inside him. "I told you at the bar—I'm home because I have to work in the morning."

"Ahhh yeahh," he said, but he didn't remember her saying that. She probably did, though. He stumbled on the skateboard, but caught his balance.

"What are *you* doing?" she asked.

"I'm just goin' back home. . .not drivin' though—I got my skateboard. Imma play some music, some stuff! But yeah we should hang out soon. . . when did you say you could again?"

"Tuesday."

"Really? You can't maybe like tomorrow?"

"I dunno...maybe."

Max opened the door to his beach house and went into his bedroom, where he kept most of his music equipment. He'd just gotten a new microphone. He told her that he'd just set it up that morning.

She showed interest, asked questions about his music, asked to listen to it, and he was floating, floating in her song of laughter and the drumming beats humming through his speakers.

He told her that he wanted to make something of himself, even when everyone thought he was just some fucked-up drug addict, even in high school. He was. But he was gonna get somewhere. He would, someday. He had an old drum set, but he could never use it at the house because of the neighbors. Again, someday he would be free to play whenever he wanted.

"I—I know this soun'z like, arrogant but I'm making something of myself and I've lived, like, everywhere and I *showed* those people in my town me and brother and, yeah." Then he started rapping to some artist's music that he produced. He asked her if she liked it. She just said yeah and listened. He imagined her nodding and smiling and genuinely loving the songs just because she was that kind of girl—always finding the good in something not so good. Finding the extraordinary in the ordinary.

After 'bout twenty minutes on the phone, he asked, "How are you dealing with me righ' now? I don' make *any* sense."

She said something about having dealt with many drunk people in the past. It was her constant job to be patient. So he kept rapping. She kept listening. Even to the nonsense about how they would go together like PB&J—she should have hung up.

But she didn't. She stayed on the phone. And she kept fucking listening. She didn't even know him, but put up with his flaws and fucked-upness already.

He kept telling her to go on his Instagram and follow him, and she did. Eventually, he said something about hanging up for five minutes. So she did. He forgot to call back.

He didn't remember that conversation the next day, when he met her for the second time.

But she was just as extraordinary, and he was just as honest.

Things had changed since then.

Tap, tap, tap.

He turned off the vacuum. Was that a knock?

Tap tap tap.

He swung the door open. "What're you *doing* here?"

Nura wore a black t-shirt and pants. Her hair was damp and her eyes wide and bare—no make-up. Pure, clean, tear-filled. "Look, I just need to talk."

"No no, just go, I don' need a girl righ' now—" He started to close the door. She stopped him.

"*Max*."

"What? What do you want?" He asked, holding onto the door and ready to close it again.

He'd been ignoring her for a week. It was the end of August anyway—no more summer flings. She was acting weird last weekend, saying some stuff about being concerned for him and his drug issues. He was okay with her caring, but she seemed to care too much.

And if girls cared too much, he would drive them crazy. He sure did with the last one; she'd moved away and would message him now and again about how he ruined her life. Sure, he was an asshole, but he didn't ruin her life. Besides, she was just as fucked up as him—snorting coke in his bathroom every night and day and tryin' to move her shit in his place.

But Nura was sweet. *Is* sweet.

"I just wanna talk," she said. He paused, trying not to feel so bad for her and just give in. But only for a second. He started to shut the door again, but she stuck her foot in and yelled.

"I'm pregnant you *asshole*!"

Max loosened his grip on the door. "What? No you're not."

She scoffed. "Uh, *yeah*. I took a fucking test. *Twice*."

He poked his head out the door to see if there were cameras and he was on some

Punk'd show.

Nope.

"Come in."

Chapter 6: Sober Water

A rippling mirror
pours over us
cold and pure
for the first time
he sits beside me
with senses
attuned to mine
his usual, drunken waves
sobered enough
to only touch
my sand skin

- *Nura Hart*

Whenever I see that sea color blue, my mind can't help but sway toward him—his eyes. Salty waves of the ocean crash onto the rocks and carve through the sand the way his kisses sink into my skin and lips.

Those eyes burst into shocked, silent waves when I tell him I'm pregnant.

And he shuts off his speakers. That's how I know it's bad. His music is constantly on in the background.

We're sitting on opposite sides of his grey bed. He's rambling now, trying to make sense of how I could be pregnant. He paces around the room and ran his fingers through his already messy hair.

"This has never happened to me I'm always careful like I swear to *god* I never came in you."

He throws his hands in the air. "You must've—did you lie about being on birth control?"

My face grows hot. "*No*! Why would you think I would do that? I don't want a baby either."

He pauses. Nods. “I know. I know you wouldn’t, but that doesn’t make sense, I—” it goes on like this for about five minutes until he finally sits back on the bed. It’s silent for a solid minute before I tell him.

“I’m not keeping it.”

He stares at the ground while he speaks. “Yeah, I can’t have a kid anyway. Like, I don’ have the money for that and I—yeah.” He knows he wouldn’t be a good father. I know that too. “But, you know. So do you need money? I don’t know how much abortions costs or what your insurance is but I can definitely pay for whatever and. Okay. Just, don’t tell anyone about this, especially your parents. Just keep it between us because if other people get involved they try to make your decisions and it gets more complicated.” He flings his hands up in the air. “Why aren’t you talking? I’m like tryin’ to figure this out and you’re quiet and just—what do you wanna do?”

I don't say anything because I realize he forgot. He forgot my parents are dead.

He turns to me, his eyes rippling—sober waters. My voice comes back from deep shock, appealing to his soft waves, crawling toward him. My own fears drift away like grains of sand along the beach.

"I'll call the doctor tomorrow. Get an appointment."

He nods. "Okay."

I stand up and grab something from my bag. A square magnet with the words "Everything will be okay in the end. If it's not okay, it's not the end." I got it for him before we broke up, hoping it might remind him of hope once in a while. I guess it was now or never. "Here, I never got to give this to you."

He takes it with his long fingers. The corner of his lip curves up. "Thanks. I'll put it on the fridge."

And that's enough for me to feel the bubbles of happiness I always feel with him. "I guess I should go now."

He stands up with me. "It's gonna be okay, okay?" Tears well up in my eyes, looking into his blue ones, waiting for him to kiss me and hold me. "Hey hey, no tripping, okay?"

He wraps his arms around me and I breathe hard against his white t-shirt. His cool, sweet scent a familiar reminder of calmness and comfort.

He rubs his hand up and down my back and whispers to me, "Don't worry I'm gonna be there, okay, good Max is here, okay, good Max is here."

I hope he stays.

Chapter 7: Dead Cat Baby

Cat cadaver
pale white and pink
wet, permanent marker odor
skin and guts and bones
sliced open
to a little purple alien
curled up in its dead
underdeveloped skin
never fully alive.

- *Nura Hart*

The last time I was at Planned Parenthood I got the pill.

And now I'm here to get rid of what the birth control was supposed to goddamn prevent.

The glass door opens. My heart jumps and I turn, but it's just some girl with nervous eyes and messy hair. That's what every girl in here looks like.

There aren't guys here. And Max still isn't here, but the nurse hasn't called me in just yet. I arrived a little early, not wanting to take a chance and miss my appointment. I slump back into the stiff, brown polka-dot armchair, then take out my phone. I replay the voicemail he left me yesterday when I texted him my appointment time: Tuesday, August 8th, at 4:30pm.

"Hey. . . it's Max uhm yeah I could probably cruise with you tomorrow. I get off work at four, uhm. . . and . . . if I don't, if I don't give you a ride or I can't get there by four or whenever it is then I'll just come straight there and, and just meet you there so I can be there for you. Uhm. . . but yeah call me back or text me when you get this and we'll talk and figure this out. Okay, bye."

Tears glop from my eyes. I manage to breathe and hold back too many tears so none of the other girls feel sorry for me or try to ask if I'm okay. Because I am okay, I'm just so moved by Max's uncanny ability to be the guy that I thought he could be: the good guy, the one who could be there. I want it, I always have. But he chooses when and where he is going to be that guy. He's never one or the other.

But it makes me happy that my instincts about him weren't completely off.

I stare at the clock just across from my chair. It's four twenty, and he still isn't here. Anxious claws tighten around my heart and lungs—*he's not coming*, I think. *But what about me? He promised. He's been good lately. He wouldn't go that far, would he?*

It's four twenty, of course he's not here, stupid bitch. He probably went to get high before coming here.

He probably took some Xanax too because he's so fucking anxious.

A white girl with long, wavy hair and wide, clueless eyes sits in a chair next to me and her left leg shakes up and down as she taps the chair's arm with her finger. The sound is as annoying as the fucking Asian torture thing where they drop water in-between your eyes. I want to yell and tell her to stop because she's making me more anxious than I already am, she's making me *violent*. I imagine grabbing her hand and slapping it on her thigh so hard she won't even be able to move either because they'll be *broken*.

"Andrea?" A short, Hispanic nurse peeks out the door to the appointment rooms with a small smile. The girl next to me rises and leaves. *Thank God.*

A pamphlet left on her chair about unexpected pregnancies taunts me.

KNOW YOUR OPTIONS, it says.

Yeah, I know the fucking options. Have the baby or don't.

I do want to have kids someday, I do. But not now. Not while I'm in college getting my degree in teaching. Not when I have so much life ahead of me—I'm only *twenty-one*, for god's sake!

I still haven't told V, either. If there is anything I agree on with Max, it's that I don't want to involve anyone else. I will tell her, though. Once it's over. I look over at the entrance door: no one in sight. I glance at the clock again. It's four-thirty-five.

The nurse peeks out the door and glances at her clipboard. "Nura?"

I sigh and make my way toward her.

He's not coming.

A fly of wind blows behind me as someone opens the entrance door.

Chapter 8: Cherry

I wish
you were my first.

My first time
popped
cherry
blood

My first time
with you
pink
cherry
drops.

- *Nura Hart*

Max's beach house—white, simple, and open. He had given me a little tour, which ended in his bedroom. He turned on some music video and lay on his bed. I plopped next to him, my heart pounding.

"You wanna watch a movie or something?" He asked.

I shrugged. I didn't really care. I just wanted him to touch me the way he touched me when I first saw him at the bar: hand on my thigh, sliding just an inch under my skirt. Just thinking about it made me dizzy.

We sank into the bed, heads on the grey and white pillows. He lay behind me and spooned me into him, then threw a blanket over our bodies.

I don't know if he knew what he was doing to me. I don't know if *I* even knew. But I did know that I felt alive for the first time since I . . . since the darkness.

That's what I call it: the darkness. Or "that night." Because I can't stand to think about it as anything else, because I can only remember bits and pieces, probably because it scares the hell outta me.

Whenever I think about, I see the black blood on white stained sheets the morning after.

I remember crying, sobbing, my cheeks flushed, panties ripped off, and a glow of sunlight shining on the stained sheets as if to remind me that my innocence had been taken away forever.

Max brushed that away when his lips touched the base of my neck, when he slid his hand over my bare thigh. Drums pounded in my chest, between my legs, in my head—everywhere. I exhaled, remembering that I needed to breathe. *This is what it's supposed to feel like.*

I slid his hand off my thigh and turned to face him. I propped myself on his chest. "Uhm, so, I should probably say this before we do anything . . ."

"Yeah, okay," he said, looking up into my eyes.

My eyes shied away. I bit down on my bottom lip.

"Well, I'm a virgin."

He propped his head up on the pillow. "Wait, seriously?"

I nodded and bit my lip so hard I could almost taste the blood; I was so nervous. Not because it was a lie, but because
I didn't know how he'd feel about it. Because I basically was a virgin; I didn't really know what sex was like, or what I was supposed to do. How could I?

He let out a nervous chuckle. Like he didn't know what to say exactly. So I touched his chest and pulled on his white shirt.

"I want to do it, though. Just, not. . .well I don't want it to be just a one time thing."

This was the real part I was afraid of saying. That he wouldn't want to have sex more than once. That he wouldn't want to touch me because he didn't want the commitment of showing a virgin girl what to do and how to do it. And I wanted to explore with him, because for some reason, I knew he would know how to move with me. I wanted to find out what good sex was like.

"Oh don't worry, I want to hang more for sure," he said. We smiled. I realized that he could've easily been lying to me. But I wasn't afraid of that. I believed him wholeheartedly.

"You're really a virgin?" He asked, then kissed me.

"Yeah," I said under my breath, between kisses.

"Okay. . . we'll go slow then. . . just let me know if it hurts too much," he told me, then put his lips to mine, and touched me everywhere.

It felt like a sore pulse pushing inside me, but soft, pleasant. Not at all like that night—not at all. I wanted him to keep going. Hurt and pleasure swirled in the experience, but it seemed natural. He moaned against my ear and he whispered how sexy I was, how bad and innocent I was. We read each other's bodies like books we couldn't put down.

And when the pain became a small beat of soreness, he pressed hard one last time before he pulled out of me and went to throw away the condom. When he came back, he sat on the bed with a bong in his hand.

"Do you care if I smoke? If you don' wan' me to it's fine," he said.

I shook my head. I didn't really care when people smoked weed. And at the time, I thought that was all with him. Just weed.

I went to the bathroom afterward to pee, because V had told me that if I ever had sex I should always pee after. So I did. I dapped the toilet paper under me, then noticed plops of blood, like drops of cherry juice spilled onto the once white, unstained paper.

Later, when he came to my house to drop me off, he called me an angel. And though the drops of cherry blood told me otherwise, I believed him. I felt like it—smiling, beautiful and lovely.

Before he left, he turned around, as if forgetting something, then bent down to kiss me. “I’ll see you later.” And his lips stretched into a grin. My cheeks warmed in pink.

And I swore to myself I was not falling for him, but in fact, I anxiously dreaded the moment that I would. Because usually, by then, I would feel it.

I didn’t.

I felt bonded, even knowing that this is was just part of the summer bliss, and that I would never settle for him in the long term because he was a colossal handful of blue eyes and dark hair, one that I didn't need to hold me back. And I wouldn't let him. That's what I told myself in the beginning, at least.

But I should've known from the moment he didn't remember that he had called me, the moment he took out that bong every time we hung out at his house—the signs were there. The signs that his drug issue was bigger than either of us. It was something that only he could pull himself out of if he chose to.

And at the time, I didn't know what he'd choose.

But at the time, I was glad I'd chosen him to clean the nightmares on my sheets.

Chapter 9: White Walls

I am a stain
in this place
of pure
white

- *Nura Hart*

It's just some guy with that surfer-blond hair, short on the sides and long and high in the middle, the kind of hair that guys brush their hand through while walking up to shore with their surfboards in hand.

But the kind of guy that surprised you. The kind that actually shows up.

"This way," the nurse said, her smile encouraging me to feel safe. But my face grows hot and blood pounds in my ears. *He's not coming.*

"Yeah," I croak.

She leads me to a back room.

You cried in my bedroom, said you're late and positive, baby you're all alone now 'cause I'm—

- MAX.

Late.

He drank at work, you know, a little bit between pouring people their drinks. He worked at the bar of an Italian restaurant, and he was bored. He stood around and saw people laughing or whisper-fighting and doing everything that he wished he could do right then.

The alcohol was there. So he took a sip of vodka here and there throughout the day. But he had to leave and Jared was late to pick up his shift.

Max texted Scott, one of his best friends since high school, to meet him there and calm him down a little. Maybe get him to his senses.

He checked his phone: four-twenty.

Late.

I go out of the room.

White walls. Sterile. Too clean. Too clean for the red that spills behind closed doors. The nurse led me down the hallway, and my hands swing by my side. One foot follows the other. I pull open the door that goes to the lobby, then look up to face the women who will probably stare at me.

An ocean reaches me instead.

He stands up when his eyes crash into mine, and he pulls me in until I'm arm's length from him and holds me to his heart. He consumes me in his wave of calmness, steadiness—his presence.

And I don’t care if people are watching. I don’t care that I had walk into a white room turned red with blood, black blood. And I don’t care that he almost let me drown alone.

Because he’s here now. He helps me float again along the shore, kisses my forehead with soft tickles of water, and I’m okay. I am okay.

He doesn’t say anything, he just holds me until I pull away because I don’t want to soak his shirt with my tears. We walk out together, but I know it won’t always be this way.

Chapter 10: Sprite

Baby my music's drowning in my habits I've–

- MAX.

"I've been drinking at work," he confessed.

Sunlight seared through my car windows.

"Why?"

"I dunno. . . just bored."

"Hm. Maybe you need a new job?" she suggested. He did want a new job. He wanted to achieve a goal, anything. Music would be nice. He wanted to be like the guys in the videos he showed her, the ones who came out with one hit and become famous overnight. He'd never really told her that, but he had a feeling that Nura knew.

She just didn't say anything, out of courtesy, perhaps, or maybe so she wouldn't have to break it to him that it might not happen.

"Yeah, maybe. . ." he said, then closed the MacBook on his lap. He didn't know why he brought it, he just wanted something to distract him maybe. He felt this guilt for some reason. Maybe it was because ever since she told him that she didn't actually remember her first time having sex, which was not with him, he felt a little sick. Or maybe it was because she'd been through enough, and all this shit was just causing more drama. Drama that he didn't need. He had to break up with her.

"So where am I going?" She asked, looking away from the road.

"Just go straight."

She drove along the road beside to beach, lips pressed together. They stopped by a burger place, picking up the burgers and drinks in the drive-through.

He gave her cash to pass along the cashier. All the while, they didn't really exchange much conversation.

Until she stopped in a parking spot. And they sat in silence together.

She had the abortion. But she hadn't said a word about it. Probably because she was mad at him for being late. He wouldn't blame her, either. He was a jackass and he knew it. But he didn't want to be, at least not to her.

He couldn't ever stand to watch her break inside. He could see it, even though she averted her eyes from him. He never knew that a girl could make him feel so bad.

"So. . .what do we do?" She croaked.

He pursed his lips. "I mean…" He turned to her. "It's up to you."

She bowed her head down because she knew the end was coming, but she held her hands in her lap because she wanted to hold on. "I...I still want to...be with you."

He knew what she meant. “I just...I can’t have a girl right now. And, I dunno, it’s just...I know you’re not pregnant anymore, but…” *but I can’t*, he thinks. *I can’t be a good boyfriend. I can’t be there for you the way you want me to. I don’t need a girl right now, anyway.*

He sipped on his sprite, bubbly on his tongue, the way Nura had made him feel before, only happier. Warmer. Lighter.

But he couldn’t love.

And she deserved to be loved, without a doubt.

Sprite pt. 2

Bubbly
sugar
and spice
pops
on my tongue

sugar
of his voice
spice
of his words

yet I long
to drink more.

- *Nura Hart*

"You want some?" He offers some Sprite to me.

I shake my head.

As he sips on his drink, I sit and think about what to say next. But nothing sounds right.

I still care about you. I just want to be with you. You don't have to love me.

It's all so pathetic and desperate. And I know I have to let him go, but I don't want to. But I'm going back to school soon. It'll be my senior year at UCSD as an Education student. Meaning I'll always be busy with studying, student teaching, hanging out with friends, writing my poetry—no time to think about boys—no time to think about *Max*. I'm twenty-one and life's supposed to be fun and wild, not heartbreaking and dull. I've had enough of that.

"Can I have some water?" I ask, pointing to the small cup of water he'd ordered.

"Yeah of course. I got it for you."

"Oh. Thanks." I take the little cup and gulp it down. I shouldn't be so surprised whenever he actually thinks of me or does something nice for me, but it always does. Because he's the type that usually only thinks of what benefits him.

I know that. And I know that the kindness shouldn't automatically overshadow his selfishness, or the way he wasn't there for me.

If I'm being honest with myself, I wouldn't be surprised if he didn't care at all. I look back at him, breathing in, trying to keep the tears from even flooding in my eyes.

"Can—can we at least be friends?" I ask.

"Yeah yeah, of course." He doesn't sound so sincere. My heart cracks. I take a sip of his sprite and the bubbles pop down my throat and singe my stomach.

"Uhm, I have to go soon, so," he says. The sprite burns through me.

He really doesn't want to be with me, I think. *God.*

As I start the car up again, and I remember all the times when maybe he wanted to be with me.

I'm stuck thinking about where I went wrong. Or when I should've run away.

Chapter 11: Strawberry Vanilla Bourbon

Soaked skin
in soft strawberry
vanilla
and a taste of bourbon
so you'll inhale
sweetness
but stay addicted

~ *Nura Hart*

It was early July, close to the fourth of July, actually. I was grabbing a book for a customer at Books & Books, where I worked, when my phone buzzed: a text from Max. And to my dismay, a fist squeezed my lungs until I burst into a smile.

No, I told myself. *Stop stop stop. He's not good for you*. Still, I couldn't help but open the text right away to see what he'd said.

Hiii babeee

The extra letters in his words was undoubtedly Max, Max and his slow, smoky voice. The smell of coffee from the shop in the bookstore and soft chatter of conversation completely disappeared from my awareness. I let my heart fill up at his attention; he was thinking of me.

User:

Heyy

How are you?

Max:

Good !!

At work

It's slow

And you ?

:)

User:

I'm goood. Just have had lot of extra work this week. What's up?

Max:

Just wanted to check up

Let's chill soon

I got ur ring too

I had almost forgotten that he had my ring, and suddenly the bareness on my left right finger was prominent—like a piece of me was missing. And he had it. It had only been the second weekend we spent together. I had slept over that Saturday night and when I left, I realized I left my ring on his nightstand.

So I called. He said he'd put it somewhere safe.

I trusted him. At the time. With the ring. But with my emotions? I wasn't sure.

User:

Oh yeah, how about tomorrow? I'm gonna be working nearby until 7:30 or 8 anyway. Would you rather hang out tomorrow or Friday?

Max:

Either one !!

I'm down for tomorrow night

After work

Or before work

User:

Okay, well I have to work tomorrow morning, then I work that night until 8pm, so maybe after that?

I know since it'll be Friday night you might have plans, but I'm busy before that

Max:

Okk figure it outbreaks

Out

I'm high hold up Han

Of course. I think the real question was when was he not high? And I didn't know how I felt about it. I think what worried me more was if he would ever ditch me even when we'd made plans.

User:

I'm pretty busy today so
tomorrow night sound okay?

Max:

Okk well seeee
:)

I wanted to roll my eyes and just text him "forget it, sorry, I have plans," because I hated uncertainty. But I also believed whenever he said "we'll see" we always ended up hanging out. At the same time, I was afraid one day, one of those "we'll sees" would end in us not hanging out, and with me waiting and him never calling or never texting or never showing up.

I knew what I was getting into when I slept with Max. I knew that he would disappoint me, that he would not surprise me and turn out to be a nice guy. I knew that. But I couldn't help the fact that my heart was disappointed when I was a second choice, if that.

We ended up not hanging out that Friday night, which was exactly what I was afraid of.

So I went to bed in darkness. On a *Friday night.* Alone.

He made it up for me on Saturday night. Kind of. I stayed the night, but I didn't even ask. He suggested it. Wanted me to.

Saturday morning, I woke up pissed, but at least I had other plans that would keep me busy. I was going to see V. She was with Dan in San Clemente for the rest of the week, so she hit me up and we made plans to go out and eat and shop. Just what I needed to get my mind off Max.

I drove to San Clemente, windows down, music pumping against the speakers on full blast and the wind whipping through my hair—I could taste the sun breaking from the morning overcast and the hands of air speeding across my cheeks and urged my voice to sing out loud because I was fucking free and invisible and alive.

Of course, I had texted him that morning saying, "Okayy do you have plans tonight after work?" Because we hadn't seen each other in six days, and fear crept on my shoulder with its cold, bony hands. Fear that we were over already.

But I had forgotten all about it when I talked to V on the freeway and ate at California Pizza Kitchen, which is when I got the text.

1:11pm.

Max:

I'm not sure
I'm still here
What are your plans??
I'm down to chill after
I'm gonna be nappy
tho
Nap time

User:

Well I'm in OC right now with a friend, but I'll be home tonight
What time do you wanna chill? Cause I can drive over any time

Max:

Idk soon

I'm tired

And dunno what I'm doing tonight

User:

Okay well I won't be home till tonight so if you wanna hang out I probably won't be able to until after you get off work

But if you're too tired to hang out tonight or wanna hang out with your friends I understand so just let me know :)

I tried to implement some vicious passive aggressive venom. I knew he'd be too oblivious to pick up on it, but it felt good to send anyway.

While V and I indulged in y double scoop of ice cream in waffle cones, my phone blares out guitar chords against my back pocket. I was still in line to pay for my ice cream, so I didn't answer.

When we sat on a bench outside, I checked my missed call. Max. My heart lifted up and I smiled; my venom had done its work, hadn't it?

"Well well, look who called," I told V. We both laughed and rolled our eyes in agreement: BOYS.

So I called him back, and when he picked up, his deep voice croaky like usual, I asked him what was up.

"Hey, what're you doing?" he asked.

"I'm in OC. I told you. I won't be back until tonight probably, what're you doing?"

"Work. I'm working a double. I get off at 9:00."

"Okay, do you wanna hang out after?"

"Yeah."

"Okay… 9:00?"

"Yeah." He sighed, sounding frustrated for some reason. Maybe the venom had worked too well, or he was just tired. He sounded a little sluggish, so maybe he hadn't had a good nap.

"Okay. Have funnnn," I said, then laughed as ice cream melted all over V's fingers.

"Yeah, okay, bye," he said, then I hung up, his voice still croaky, but not really sluggish like I had originally thought, but cranky and moody and dark. *Jeez.*

I shrugged, not wanting anything to ruin my perfect girls' day.

A little bit later, right when V and I got in the car to go back to San Clemente, he texted me:

Sry I'm in a shitty mood
We'll chill later
I wasn't supposed to work a double shift

I rolled my eyes again and asked V to reply back since I started to drive already. Despite all my anger at him, I couldn't help but feel bad for him. Stupid sexy, grumpy voice. Stupid apology.

That's okay bb

we'll hangout tonight and have fun, just relax

Max:

Okay :)

I got home around seven that evening, and knew he wouldn't be off till nine, so I put on my new pair of high-waisted army shorts and black graphic tee I got at Forever 21. Then I headed out, figuring I'd kill some time reading. I texted him at nine.

User:

Lmk when you're off work

Max:

Okkk bb

Still not off

User:

Okay

It wasn't that much longer that he texted me back:

Come baby

Where r uu

I soaked my freshly-shaved and washed body in my new Bath & Body Works Strawberry Vanilla Bourbon lotion—sweet, fruity, and addictive. I took in the smell and hoped it would flow softly in the air around me. I wiped my hands of the lotion to pick up my phone.

Before I could answer his text, he called me.

"Yes?" I said.

"Hey. How far are you?"

"Like 10 or 15."

"Okay, I wanna get food. I'm super hungry."

"Okay. Like 10 minutes, okay? Be there soon."

"Okayyy bye."

I headed over, bright red and blue lights flashing by and uniformed men surrounding one car—cops in every parking lot. It was 4th of July weekend and people were partying their asses off and getting their asses pulled over; I already knew this night was gonna be interesting.

When I pulled into the gate of his house, I called him, but he didn't answer. So I got out of the car and knocked on his garage. He told me to come in and that I could park anywhere, but I knew he wanted to go out and get food. He was all over the place, that boy.

I waited for him, and I was listening to Green Day, so when he opened the car door he said, “Hey, can I drive?” I shrugged and said sure. He was a better driver than I was anyway.

“Can I play my music? I don’t feel like listening to Green Day.”

I said “yeah” automatically, mostly because I was surprised he even recognized that it was Green Day so quickly—the song wasn’t even one of their popular ones and because when he entered the car strawberry milk smoke of his vape cast me under his bad boy spell.

He adjusted the seat for his long legs and smoothed his other hand over the steering wheel. “Awh, I wanted this kind of car, actually. Kinda, you know, out my price range. . .” then he grabbed his phone and lit up the light to take a snapchat and send it to his friends, I guessed. I rolled my eyes. I did that a lot with him.

He turned then and puckered his lips to kiss me. I smiled and kissed him.

We drove to an In-n-Out, and when the line took too long, he decided to back out and go somewhere else.

“Where are we going?”

“Buy some druggssss.”

Right. Of course.

“Happy hour ends at eleven, so I gotta hurry.”

I glanced at the green numbers on the dash: 10:52.

He sped up to ninety mph, heading toward one hundred.

“*Holy*—Slow down!” I demanded, pointing at the dash. I looked out the windows, ready for a police siren to blare and to pull us over. But I’d been lucky in my short driving career. Or maybe not lucky, but consciously careful because of my father’s recklessness.

He just smiled and said, “I’m not even close to its limits.” Like that was supposed to reassure me.

I wasn’t looking to test that like my father had. I inhaled, trying to sniff for any bit of alcohol on Max. Nothing, which was good. And though I tensed during this alarming sense of danger, I couldn’t deny the sense of freedom and recklessness I felt; I wanted him to speed up, but I also didn’t want to end up like my parents, crushed against the hard metal of an abandoned car on the side of the freeway.

If we were on an empty highway, I might’ve told him to drive faster, to drive so fast that the darkness and lights would merge in a zipping blur of black night, so if we did die, I wouldn’t even see it coming. I wondered if my parents saw it coming.

But I had a sense of the line between destructive mistakes and harmless fun, Max didn't, and that's how he was still a young soul; a psychic would later tell me this, which only confirmed what I already knew.

Max could be as dangerous and reckless as my father was.

He pulled a parking lot, next to a two story, abandoned-looking building. He stopped before parking, and told me to park the car while he went inside. There was one other car there, their lights still on. They were parked in front of a spot that clearly said "DON'T YOU DARE PARK HERE" in big, red letters. Every spot had a sign like that. I figured that was just to scare people away, so I parked, but before I could adjust my awful parking job, BANG.

I jumped and turned: Max. He tapped on the window. I unlocked the door. He jumped into the passenger seat. "They're fucking closed. What the hell?" then he tapped some buttons on his phone and made a call. He asked something about them changing locations. I guess they hadn't; people were there, but they were on the second floor of the building.

"Oh, okay."

A guy came out from the building. A mere shadow, really.

"Be back," he said, then got out and grabbed his phone. My phone lit up. Max. But he was walking toward the building, so I figured he was butt dialing, so I hung up.

Ding.

Voicemail from Max Sommer.

I smiled and checked to see if he said anything in the voicemail. His deep, croaky voice mixed with static, fragments of his voice.

Nothing, just a careless accident.

My heart sank. I couldn't tell if I was sad or happy or just regretful. But I decided I wouldn't regret anything. I didn't feel the slightest guilty that I had sex with a guy like Max, or not even *like* Max, just Max. For some unreasonable reason, I wanted to stay with him for as long as I could. Maybe it had to do with that chemical connection they said you get when you have sex with someone, but I remember this feeling; I'd had it before. It's not a chemical, sexual attachment. It's an attachment that forms from committing time and effort to someone, and I was getting dangerously close to the line between caring and loving. Or maybe I'd already crossed it, and I just hadn't looked down as I ran through the paths.

I waited about fifteen minutes before he came back out. I unlocked the doors and he hopped in, smelling the bags of weed in his hand. "Awww, that's good. Smell it."

He held a bag toward my nose. I leaned forward and sniffed.

"Damn," I whispered, though I wasn't really interested.

I sat at the wheel, then looked over at him. "You wanna drive?" I asked.

He stared out the front window. "I mean—do you wanna get back faster?"

I shrugged. "Are you okay to drive?"

"Yeah, yeah." Then he got out and headed to the driver's side while I climbed over to the passenger seat.

He adjusted the seat for his long legs, then sniffed the bags one more time.

"Alrighttt. You sure you don't want food?" He said as he drove out into the street.

I nodded. "Yeah, I'm good. If you wanna get something, you can."

He debated in his head. "Yeah…we'll just go back. There's food at the house."

So we drove back, music thumping back on again. "Did you miss me?" he asked.

I smiled. “Hmmm. When? Like just now or this week?”

He didn’t answer. I wondered if he heard me or just didn’t want to know my answer. So instead of asking him again, I let it go.

He turned down the music, so I knew he was getting ready to say something. “So umm. I’m gonna probably go out to some parties after this. Just drop my off at home and we can hang out tomorrow, yeah? Like in the morning or something?”

I froze, too stuck in disbelief to even scoff at him. I was about ready to punch him.

“Yeah?” He grinned. That damn James Franco-grin.

I breathed out an almost hysterical laugh. “Uh, no.”

“You won’t hang out tomorrow?”

I crossed my arms.

“No.”

His grin grew wider. "Ahhhh I gotttherrr. Hahah, wait did you really believe me?"

I rolled my eyes and scoot away from his hand that reached out to my thigh. "Uh yeah. Jeez."

"So you would've No'd me if I did that? Would you be mad?"

"Yeah, *duh* I'd be mad."

"Like forever?"

A moment's hesitation was all it took for me to know that I couldn't say no. Not forever. Would I be able to cut him off, forever? RIP. In my chest.

"No," I admitted, sighing, "No, not forever. It's hard for me to stay mad at people. But I can hold a grudge—maybe a few days, maybe weeks."

"Oh yeah?" He reached over and rubbed my thigh with his hand. I died every time he did that. "Nah, you're staying the night baby. I mean, if you want to anyway…"

I smiled. He always asked, "You gonna stay the night?" Or "You can stay if you want."

I wondered if he was waiting for the day that I would say, "No, I can't," or if he even cared. This would be my third weekend spending the night on Saturday. Always on Saturday. And I wondered if he noticed that, too, if it was somewhat unconsciously becoming a habit for the both of us. As if we were getting used to each other's presence like your body getting used to the summer sun after months of winter.

It wasn't long after that that we arrived at his place, and he parked my car and asked again, "Did you miss me?" He turned off the engine, facing me.

I bit down on my bottom lip.

"How much did you miss *me*, scale of 1-10?" I dared to ask, figuring it was safe to ask now that he'd asked me three times.

His grin grew like the Grinch who stole Christmas, only handsome and sexy and dangerous, goddammit. And slowly, pronouncing every syllable with emphasis, "Ten. Point. One."

He puckered his lips for a kiss, his eyes closed.

I popped a kiss on his lips, then hopped out of the car and giggled, the thrill of romance and night bubbling up my mood. All his flaws were so easily forgotten.

We walked down the street toward his house, arms tangled together. "So how was your day?" He asked.

The question took me by surprise; he didn't really usually ask about me. At least, not often, and not like that.

"It was fun. You know, saw my friend in San Clemente, caught up with her. Did some shopping. Ate good food."

"Ahh a little road trip, huh?"

"Yeahhh," I shrugged. We got to the doorstep and I dropped my stuff in his room before following him into the kitchen upstairs. Music blasted from the back room, his mother's room, but Max didn't seem to think it was weird. He just went upstairs to make food. The boy was always starving it seemed.

He opened the fridge and started pulling food out; some cheese, meat, then crackers from a cupboard.

"So how was work?" I asked, leaning on the kitchen counter with my phone in one hand.

"Ahh, long. I worked from eleven today."

"Damn," I said.

"Yeahh. How was yourrrr day?" he asked again, looking back in the fridge for more food.

"You already asked me," I said, but I answered again anyway because I liked that he asked. "It was fun. Really fun."

He turned around, and took a bite of the crackers and cheese. “Good.”

I went to the clear cabinet with the glasses in it to pour myself some water. He came over and wrapped his arms around me, his head buried in my hair.

“You smell good,” he said.

I smiled, thinking that I was glad I’d soaked myself in the Strawberry Vanilla Bourbon lotion. But whatever I did, whatever I smelled like, tasted like, acted like—none of it would be enough for him in the end.

And maybe I should be happy about that.

Chapter 12: A Blonde Dream

Hope floods in
like golden sunlight
from the windows
breaking from the clouds
to reach you and tell you
that you can live
without him
you can love
without him
the sun will keep
shining
golden dreams
alive.

- *Nura Hart*

I tell V about Max on the car ride to our apartment near UCSD. It's the day after Max and I talked in the car and . . well. Broke up. Uhg. FUCK.

It's a bright day, though I don't feel the cheeriness that we pass by on the road along the beach. Kids run around with sand stuck to their bodies after dipping in the ocean, couples hold hands and walk along the shore, girls lay in their bikinis and soak in vitamin D, or skin cancer.

V drops her jaw in shock when I tell her about how Max broke up with me. I don't tell her about how I got an. . . but I tell her that I had a pregnancy scare. And Max's reaction. Then I tell her how we were supposed to go out after not hanging out for a week. And he was late. Again. Probably because he just had to get high first.

And he didn't want to be together anymore.

We pass by rows of houses that block the view of the beach and shadows loom over me.

"Are you okay? That's a stupid question, actually, I'm sorry." She pats my shoulder.

I shake my head and shrug. "I dunno. I just—I miss him."

She scrunches her lips to the side and nods in understanding. "Yeah that makes sense, and Max is a jackass. Like who. . . I mean, he can just go to hell. He obviously still has a drug problem, too."

We pull into the parking lot, and our apartment complex looks like most of the housing around San Diego; rough, tan stone with palm trees standing around the front entrance, and a community pool.

"Yeah, you're right." I sigh and get out of the car, hoping that maybe some manual labor will distract me from the fucking waves of pain squeezing the veins and arteries around my heart. Is this what a heart attack feels like?

I try to focus on the thrill on moving V's stuff into the apartment. She'd been at her parents in San Diego for the summer after our junior year, out of the dorms. So
I got the apartment for me to live in the summer and for her to move in with me when school starts up in September.

V opens up the trunk and groans at the piles of boxes we have. And this was only the first load of crap we had to get from storage.

This is what you end up with when you have too much baggage.

"Dan's at soccer practice so we're on our own for now, but his friend Scott's gonna help in a bit! He's actually transferring to UCSD this year. And he's kinda cuteeee." V winks and lugs up one of her boxes to the apartment.

I roll my eyes and pick my own box. "How does he know Dan?"

"They were friends before Dan moved to San Clemente for High School. Scott's from San Diego, actually. He's nice!"

I nod and just get to moving.

We work diligently. The sun burns through my dark hair and sweat drips down to my forehead, but it feels good. Like the people on the beach, I can soak in the heat, let it dig in my skin and distract me from any thought other than *hot*. Damn, it is hot.

We're about halfway done with the boxes when V shouts, "Oh! Scott's downstairs. He has my couch in the trunk!" She jumps to the door, her long legs easily walking over the boxes scattered on the floor. I'm excited because I'd been living that summer without a couch, not that I would've really used it anyway. With all the hours that I work, I just need a place to sleep and eat.

We go downstairs to meet Scott, and when we reach the lobby, I stop dead.

Golden hair and butterscotch eyes—striking features I've seen before. From the Planned Parenthood. He smiles at me without a sign of recognition.

"Hey!" V greets Scott with a hug and smiles as she introduces us. "Nura, this is Scott," V introduces. "Scott, Nura."

I stick my hand out, hoping I can hide my nervousness. "Nice to meet you," I say. He takes my hand, which envelopes over mine, and smiles. And damn is that some smile.

"You too."

I part my hand from his as sweat balls up in my palms. I wish that it wasn't so damn hot outside now. I can't stop sweating. *Oh god, does he recognize me? Or pretending not to but really does?*

I steer my eyes away from his, hoping he doesn't recognize me.

"Alright, let's get this couch," V says, and just as she walks out, I take the moment to tap Scott on the shoulder, though I have to reach because he's freakishly tall.

"Hey. . . uhm. . ." I don't know how to go about it.

His lips curve up just slightly, and he nods. "It's okay. I won't tell." His right dimple, combined with his light hair in the glow of sunlight, somehow makes me believe that he's part of some golden blonde dream, and maybe there's some hope within that light.

Chapter 13: Popcorn chocolate

She say I'm her bae and momma likes her so I guess that's okay as long as I can fuck her kiss her maybe even feed her breakfast go to Memphis but—

- MAX.

Nura met Max's mother about in mid-July, when things were getting a little more serious. For Nura, at least.

His mom came upstairs while Nura and Max went through the food in the fridge for something to cook. She smiled with a plastic Ziploc in her hand. Blonde, beautiful even with the wrinkles under her eyes.

"Hi, I'm his mom," she said with a white, kind smile.

"Hi," Nura said, then waved only to realize Max's mom was a little tipsy; she swayed with every step and put a hand on Max's shoulder.

She stared at the food Max had in front of him, then turned to me. "Are you hungry? Did Max offer you something to eat?"

"Oh yeah, he offered, I'm just not hungry," Nura said. She never seemed to eat that much, at least around Max. He noticed, so he'd always offer her something. She usually didn't take up on that offer.

His mom pursed her lips then nodded.

"How drunk are you?" Max asked, laughing a little.

She smiled. "How do you know?"

"You always play this song when you're gone," he mused.

"Yeah, he's good isn't, he?"

"A fucking legend."

Max smiled at Nura, thinking about how beautiful she looked right then with her dark hair falling on her bare shoulders in a messy wave and her thighs and ass filling her camo-green shorts.

He pat his mom on the shoulder and pointed to Nura. “So what do you think of this girl, Mom? Pretty, huh? I found her on the street corner.”

Nura’s mouth formed an O and she reached across the counter and shoved Max’s shoulder. “You’re so mean!” she said.

His mom gasped. "Max, don't say those things! I raised you better than that! Don’t be so rude.”

Nura shook her head at him. They watched his mom circle around the table and look out the window.

“I just got back from a Cat Power concert,” she said. “Do you know Cat Power?” she asked Nura as she got out a joint and lighter.

Nura shook my head. “No, I don’t.”

Her mouth fell open. “Oh, my gosh, look her up, you would like her!”

“Yeah, I’ll do that.”

Max watched Nura type something in her phone, maybe looking up Cat Power, or maybe a little uncomfortable.

“Mom—” Max said, “She doesn’t want—“

“No, I think you’d like her. Max, don’t you know she would like that? You should listen to her, she’s so great!”

“Okay, yeah, I’ll look her up.” Nura said, and she seemed to actually be typing in Cat Powers.

“Do you want some?” Mom offered Max and Nura her joint.

“No, I don’t want that crap. I got better shit,” Max said. Mom looked to Nura.

“I’m alright,” she said.

“She doesn’t really smoke,” Max said.

Mom flushed and frowned. "Oh, I'm sorry. Am I bothering you? I'll go." She started heading toward the stairs, but Nura shook her head.

"No no, it's okay. I don't mind. I smoke sometimes, just not now."

"Oh no, it's okay… I don't wanna bother you kids."

"No, Mom, we wanna hang out with you," Max insisted. Nura's lips hitched up. They both smiled at each other, and maybe, just maybe, he thought he could see her in his life for a little longer than he planned. Mom smiled, then, with the blunt in-between her fingers, headed back downstairs anyway.

"Sorry, she's kind of drunk," Max apologized as he went back into the kitchen.

"No, she's nice," Nura said, tracing the counter and staring at the fruit in the fruit bowl.

"Yeah, she's pretty chill. I wish I was more like her, though—she always sees the positive in everything and, like, people are just attracted to her. People like her," he said, opening the fridge and thinking about how he really did wish that he could be more like her. And how she was the only person really there for him throughout his life. It was his mom, she had to be, but not always, at least not with the way he had behaved in the past, right?

Who the hell knows, he thought. He focused back on finding something to eat instead when his phone buzzed in his back pocket.

Scott—huh, he hadn't heard from him in a while, but he heard he was back in town from college.

You comin tonight?

Max:

Where at?

Scott:

My place—got dope shiit

Max looked over at Nura, leaning on the bar and scrolling through her phone, her breasts straining against her tank top.

Got a girl over

so tmr

Scott:

nice

He dug out some chocolate from the side shelf, some good stuff from Trader Joe's. He took a bite of the popcorn chocolate, which popped on his tongue with a blast of butter and melted in the sweet, creamy chocolate.

"Mmmm, this shit is so good. I got like three different flavors, and you wouldn't think that popcorn chocolate would be the best, but it was actually the best out of alllll of them—wanna try?" He offered me some to Nura, wondering if she would take some food this time. She broke off a piece while eyeing a bottle of white wine by the sink.

She stuck the piece of chocolate in her mouth, her glossy lips closing around them. Lips that he wanted to kiss again and again.

"*Mmmmm*, *wow*, that's *so* good," she said.

"Right?" He leaned over to grab another piece, hovering over her. "Probably real good like, after sex."

She bit down on her bottom lip and broke into a smile. "Oh, I bet."

He leaned in and kissed her real quick, then put the chocolate back in the fridge. She picked up the bottle of wine she'd been eyeing. "What's this?"

"You want some?"

"Yes, I would." She went over to get a glass from the cabinet and the white wine in the glass and gulped up half of it in one motion. Her cheeks blushed almost immediately.

She leaned on the other side of the counter, across from him. He looked at her eyes, twinkling with gold, then down her shirt. He started to pull her top down, his phone pointed at her breasts.

"Stoooppp,"she said in that playful tone with underlying seriousness in it, though she didn't lift her shirt to stop him. She liked to tease.

"No, no, it's sexy," he smiled again, then adjusted her shirt to show more boob and half her bra while he snapped more pictures. She just rolled her eyes and smiled.

He put his phone down and grabbed the bottle of wine, and poured the rest in a tall, glass cup. He filled it about halfway. Nura gulped up the rest of hers while he chugged his. The spin of alcohol warped them in a warm blanket, and Nura's pink cheeks spread across her face.

They laughed and suddenly the night stirred with wine and kisses and touching and sex. Sweet and melting together with the pop of alcohol and weed and whatever else he decided to take that night, then spend some time with whatever girl he was with.

This time, it was Nura. And this was how it was with her, every night they spent together. They would talk some, kiss some, sleep in the bed and have sex if he wasn't too fucked up.

They went downstairs to his room, falling into the bed together. He wrapped his arms around her and smoothed his hands on every curve of her body, from her thigh to her ass, to her hips, her waist, her breasts, her shoulders, her neck. He could remember every one.

He was getting used to having her there every weekend. He liked it. He liked *her*. Locks of hair and dark eyes like the chocolate that turned gold in the sun, gold like buttered popcorn.

He wanted her for longer than he thought he would.

Chapter 14: Drought

Salt stings
as the sun
crusts
my skin dry
lips chapped
without you
to cool me
brush me
with water
your water—
gone
dry
a damned drought.

- *Nura Hart*

I close the window so the shade will cool my sweaty skin. V's half-way moved in already, but I stop to listen to music and lay on my room floor. And it's just me. Just me.

I feel like the earth would feel if it was torn apart from its oceans—dried brown. Dead.

I want to be cooled with a wash of water, ocean water showering over me. Replenish me and let me soak in the sun's rays with open arms instead of dry dread. The ocean. I needed it, I need it to be with me. Without it, I'm just hot late-August sand that people cannot bear to walk on.

Being apart from him cuts the center of my heart more and more every day. Deeper, sinking through every vein, every source of life. I don't think he ever really understood how much I loved, *do* love, him. Or maybe he does and he just never said anything.

When I was with him, I never felt the need to express it in words, because I was calm with him. Sane, at peace. I could fall along with his waves and get my fill of highs and lows. He made me forget. . . forget. . .

The darkness. With him, I could forget that night ever happened. That the shadow never stripped me down and made me bleed. Black blood. Max made it go away; he washed it away so I wouldn't have to look at that blood again.

He's the addiction I can't shake off.

I never thought I would understand how Bella felt when Edward left her in *Twilight*. But I do now. I do. And yes, it's just as pathetic.

I feel high as SoundCloud rappers spit out lyrics through my speakers. I turn up the volume and suck in air that suddenly smells like him—vanilla smoke—and I'm afraid that I'll forget he ever existed.

Tears gush out from my eyes and onto my carpet in fat, hot globs of salt water. And I'm aware of how pathetic I am.

Believe me, I know. I try to shut my brain when I hear that music and think "Max always listened to this" because I should stop thinking about him. Or I'll never be able to get over him.

Tap tap tap.

I jump up and pretend to be making my bed when I say, "Come in!"

V peeks into the dark room and laughs. "Haha, is it not dark enough in here?"

I shrug and smile. "Just trying to cool down."

"Smart, actually," Scott says from behind. V widens the door and my body stops functioning as I look at him again and remember where saw him. And I realize something.

He didn't just see me there, but I saw *him* there. Why was he at Planned Parenthood? Did he get a girl pregnant too?

"You still coming to IKEA with us?" V asks.

I nod, then shake off my suspicions about Scott. It's not any of my business. Plus, he said he wouldn't tell. But is it because he doesn't want to explain why he was there too?

As we walk to his truck downstairs, I try to let it go, but something about him seems off. *Feels* off. Maybe it's the way he smiles, and how bright and full that smile is against his sun-kissed tan, too bright to be true.

When we arrive at IKEA and V goes to the bathroom, Scott breaks the tension.

"So I'll tell you why I was there if you tell me."

The cracks on my chapped lips split as I try to find the words to explain what I lost. I clear my throat, but my voice still comes out a little croaky.

"Honestly, I don't really care why you were there. I'm not gonna say anything to V about it," I tell Scott, crossing my arms. Who is he to ask anyway?

I look away from him and my eyes wander toward the aisles of furniture. I see little pillows shaped like elephants, and I wonder if they have any dolphins or turtles.

The corner of his lips hitch up as he nods. “Right. Sorry. It’s none of my business. It’s just—well, nevermind.”

V waves over at us. I’m thankful for her interference. “Thanks for waiting! Alright, let’s pick out our stuff.”

“Cool,” I say, then clear my throat again, but it is still scratchy and dry.

Like I’m stuck in a drought.

Chapter 15: Black ocean

xannies in my system time to get clean but—

Fuck.

- Max.

A film of sweat formed on his forehead and the back of his neck. Though it was mid-July, he wasn't sweating because of the heat.

His hands shook as he held the bong in his hand and put it back on the ground. His eyes drooped and body slugged its way down on his bed right after smoking a bowl or two, or however many he had. He tried to put his Xannies away for a couple of days now.

It was day three. The heat didn't help much. He just needed to sleep. That was all. He turned on his fan on full blast and turned on some music, the soft beat pressing into his ears like a soft lullaby.

Sleep.

Detox.

He snapchatted her, and she responded, but he didn't say anything after. She texted him, too. He didn't respond. He couldn't.

And just as he resolved to close his eyes, his phone rang.

Nura.

He let it ring and turned to his side, then pushed away the blankets that stuck to his skin.

Ring ring ring ring ring

He groaned and looked at his phone. Nura. Again. He hung up again, then texted her so she'd stop:

Im fine I just have a cold rn

So I've been sleeping

Nura:

jesus you scared the crap out of me

sorry sometimes I get a bad feeling
about stuff then get anxious

Max:

Ok I'm gonna pass out
Talk to u late r

He tossed his phone to the side of the bed. Maybe he didn't want to be with her as long as he thought.

His body ached and begged for some rest. His eyelids fell over the salty sweat stinging his blue eyes. He welcomed the blackness.

A few days later, he wiped the tables with a white cloth so hard that he knocked a chair over and everyone stared. *Did she really have to work that much?* Maybe Nura'd been annoying the other day, but that didn't mean he wanted her to fuck around with other guys. So he texted her later that week, asking if she could hang out.

She had to work.

Then he asked about tomorrow.

She said maybe, depending on whether she had to work again.

Finally, he threw his towel on the bar. "Mario, I'm taking my break!" he called out, not waiting for an answer.

He went outside of the Italian restaurant, which was filled with only a light crowd. Just a few older women enjoying colorful happy hour drinks, nothing too wild. Yet.

He called her. Waiting.

Waiting.

Wait. . . ing . . .

No answer.

He hung up, a little annoyed, but just as he was about to go back inside, his phone buzzed.

“Hey, what’s up?” she said, cheery, as if the time that they hadn’t spent together didn’t faze her at all.

“What’re you doing?”

“Nothing. What about you?”

“Just at work—”

“Aye! How long is that break gonna be?” Mario called out from out the door, though he wasn’t angry. He could just be a loud guy sometimes. Max held the phone closer to his ear.

“Just a sec! Sorry,” he shouted at

Mario, then turned his attention back to Nura on the phone: “What’re you doing later?”

“Uhm...I dunno.”

"Wanna chill?"

A pause. He heard some background noise; voices. Sounded like women, though, so he didn't worry too much.

"Yeah, sure."

"Okay. I get off at four. I'll text you."

"Okayy. Have fun at work." She seemed to warm up a little, her voice bubbly and grounding at the same time. He smiled; he had nothing to worry about. This girl liked him.

"Okay, baby. Bye."

Chapter 16: Golden Silk

hot pressure
sucks oxygen
from my breath
his touch
forms diamonds
on my skin
threads
my lips
into silk—
lips between
my thighs
hands on
my curves
weaving me
into gold—
carving me
into art.

- *Nura Hart*

He made me wait, again. It'd been more than a month of us seeing each other. I think two months now actually, and I was tired of it. But this time I made my anger clear.

And this time, he made his jealousy clear.

It seemed that I wasn't the only one who felt insecure.

I only had twenty more minutes of my shift at the bookstore, so I texted him and asked where he was. He said he was at a friend's house. I told him I'd be off in twenty minutes.

He didn't text back.

So when I closed up the store, I waited for the buzz in my back pocket, and the anticipation built in my chest like ton after ton of weight. I worried.

I shelved back some books, one after the other with careful precision. I put *IT* by Stephen King into its place, and sighed when I had no more books. I checked my phone, even though I knew it would've buzzed if he had texted.

No messages.

Ten minutes later, when I could find nothing else to do to give him more time, I called. He picked up.

"Hey, what're you doing?" I asked.

"I'm at my friend's house right now. Can you come in like, uhm, twenty minutes?" I sighed and shook my head, but I needed to get some gas anyway, so I said I didn't mind.

"I'll see you."

"See you baby."

I hung up and marched to my car, my purse banging against my thigh in an furious batter. Once I got inside the Lexus, I cranked up my music: loud, obnoxious rock.

I wanted to *scream* at him. *Why are you making me wait all the fucking time? You know what? Let's not hang out. If you can't make time now, we won't have time at all.*

I drove across the street to get some gas when he texted me. I thought about not answering.

Hey baby

Where are you?

I'm still chillin

Wanna come soon tho?

I rolled my eyes and didn't answer. I pushed the gas nozzle in my car and thought about crushing my phone so he could never call me again. Or maybe I would just block him so I could still keep my phone.

Whatever.

DA DA DUN, DA DA DA DA DA DA DUN DA DA

I jumped as my ringtone blasted out and the gas pump popped up. My hands shook. Max. Calling.

Darling you got to let me know, should I stay or should I go?

I sighed. *I guess I'll stay for now.*

"Hello?" I didn't bother to hide the bitter sting in my voice.

"Hey, you coming? Do you know where it's at?"

"Uhm, yeah. Just give me like, ten

minutes, okay?" I grabbed the gas nozzle and put it back into its place.

"What? Why?"

"I just need ten minutes."

"Why? Who're you with?" his voice got urgent, paranoid, even. I rolled my eyes even though he couldn't see.

"No one."

"Are you with some guy?"

"No, I—"

"I swear to God, if—"

"Max. I'm not. I'm just getting gas,

Jesus."

Silence. I jumped back into my car and slammed the door. I sighed again, and I could feel the headache start to come on from the stress of him. Of waiting. Of trying to convince him that I wasn't some cheater, although it gave me some satisfaction to know that he would be afraid of that. Good. *Maybe he should be a little scared of losing me for once.*

"Okay. Well, I sent my location, but do you want me to stay on the phone with you to direct you? Which gas station are you at?" his gravelly voice smoothed to a steady wave, comforting, and maybe even caring.

I couldn't help but smile.

"I'm at the one by Books & Books."

"Okay, so, take a left."

He directed me the whole way back to where he was, which was just across the street from his actual house. I drove into this trailer park and told him I was there.

I waited.

And waited.

In pitch-black, except for my car lights. I almost screamed when someone in a white t-shirt appeared, but then I realized it was him. The guy I'd been waiting for.

His sweet and minty aroma filled the car when he sat in the passenger seat, as if the air announced his arrival.

He smiled, "Hey baby." Kissed me. "Thanks for picking me up." He put a hand on my thigh and I blushed. Then I remembered how I was supposed to be mad at him. So I frowned.

"Yeah, okay," I said.

"Are you mad?"

I glared into his blue eyes—*dammit.* They glistened like a crying ocean, like he was sad that he actually upset me. I turned my head away and drove back onto the road leading to his house.

"Aw, I'm sorry...I made you wait a long time, huh?"

I scoffed. “Yeah.”

“I know you’ve been seeing other guysssss,” he accused.

“How would you know?”

“I just knowww.”

And for some reason, the satisfaction of making him jealous made my heart brave. My stomach filled up to my chest as I asked what I always wanted to ask him. “Do you not want me to?”

He sighed and flashed a little half smile. “Well, not really. I mean I’m not seeing other girls.”

Max may have cared more than he let on. Or maybe it was just the drugs and alcohol talking.

I nodded. “Okay. I wasn’t seeing anyone anyway.”

He put a hand on my thigh and directed me back to his house, which I could've figured out if I hadn't been thinking about the warmth that spread through me when he touched me, and how my skin felt the loss when he let go. So I held his arm as we walked to his house, streetlights guiding the path, ocean whistling kisses to my ears.

We stumbled inside and went upstairs to drink a couple beers together at the table with a paisley flower table cloth.

I texted V back about some prank she pulled on Dan, but Max took my phone and smiled.

"Who're you textingggg?" he teased, then began a text back to V. I snatched it from him before he could.

"It's just one of my friends." I smiled. I finished my text and put my phone down. As soon as I did, Max took it and got on Snapchat. "Hey, stop!" I reached for the phone, but he raised his hand out high. He was so much taller than me. Not fair.

"What? You can look at my phone, here." He tossed his phone to me, the screen open. The unread notifications blared on the screen in read.

I could do it.

I could read everything, he said. But I didn't want to take advantage of it. Or maybe I was just afraid of what I'd find.

So I tossed him back the phone as he took snapchats on mine. He tried to get a video of us together but I kept hiding from the camera; I looked awful with my messy work hair, wrinkled black tank top, and half-melted makeup.

"Wow, you look even cuter than me," he said as I wrapped my arm around his shoulders. Heat pressed into my cheeks and I pushed him playfully.

"*Stawwp.*" I laughed and pulled him off of the chair.

"Okay okay, you can delete them if you want," he said, handing me back my phone. I didn't really care, though, because I liked that he was getting jealous. That he wanted me to be his. I wanted him to be mine.

We kissed, then toppled downstairs to his bedroom. Beer sloshed in my belly and buzzed through my brain, making me a little loopy and giggly.

We fell onto the grey sheets. He stroked his fingers across my arms, through my hair, and let out a heavy sigh as he closed his eyes. I pushed his hand away and giggled. He smiled, his cheekbones sinking in with it.

"You knoww I—I care 'bout you, right?" he slurred.

I touched his arm.

"No," I croaked. I crossed my arms so I would stop touching him.

He put his hand on my hip and pulled me closer to him, our bodies fitting together the way bodies should fit together. The way sand and water would always fit together, the sand yielding to the water as it carved through it and kissed it and beat it.

"I do, though. I care. About you. Thanks for being so loyal to me baby." He kissed me again, and the soft remnants of cool and sweet mint smoothed over my tongue, then dissolved, making me pull in deeper for more.

He was always good at that: making me want more. Because the world tasted too plain, like still air, without him.

He grabbed his vape, and after inhaling chemicals in his vape, soft clouds of vanilla smoked into me as our mouths tangled together.

His lips brushed my glossy legs, circling to my inner thighs. His hand smoothed over my breasts, and belly; his tongue licked the creamy flow that spilled at his command. A shiver of pleasure tickled down my spine. I longed for a deeper kiss, and he did. And when his tongue slipped down my Vanilla Strawberry Bourbon-soaked skin, he drank me in, savoring every flavor, drunk off the sweet bourbon. Sweet fruit and alcohol and vanilla sent us into euphoric heaven.

His hands circled and squeezed down my body, so soft, like he was weaving me into gold. Into gold, with his calloused, worn palms, palms that held a young, silky, tight body. My body. It belonged with his bone and muscle, the soft and plump curves. Someone damaged as much as he was on the inside. Not poisoned with drugs, but pure water to clean his polluted ocean.

This was how it felt every night I spent with him.

Like he weaved me into gold.

Carved me into art.

To feed him. Clean him.

But he may have just poisoned me.

Chapter 17: Mango Strawberry

Mango peels into yellow
like a ball of sun
and strawberry sprinkles
dip into the pool
of blue
as golden yellow
falls into the world
and ends
another day
and perhaps
night will stay as sweet
as the mango strawberry sunset

- *Nura Hart*

It's when I'm next to Scott, just us two, that I realize I've seen him somewhere before. Other than Planned Parenthood. I just can't figure out where.

Sand cushions my body as I sit next to him on the beach, watching the sunset while V and Dan dare each other to go into the water. Scott and I opted out. I tried not to be too annoyed with that because he was a nice guy, and he did help with the move-in. It wasn't his fault I wanted to be alone. Plus, V thought he was alright.

We sat in silence for a little bit, just watching the lines of water ripple toward the horizon. Children's laughter sings in my ears like notes in the cool, evening breeze, giving the day's last bit of life before it ends. For a while, I feel at peace. And though the back of my throat still feels dry, I'm near the ocean, and I breathe in its damp, salty air. And I miss him, but at least I'm a little closer to him now.

"I was there for Max," Scott says out of nowhere.

What?

My ears perk up at Scott's confession, though I'm not sure that I heard him right.

"What?"

Scott's eyes meet mine. His eyebrows are knit together, lips in a straight line.

"How do you know Max?" I ask.

"We've been friends since high school. Our parents knew each other. Hadn't talked in a while, though. The last time we talked was a few months before he told me about you. We went to a party at UCSD, actually. Anyway, the next thing I know, he calls me and tells me he's freaking out about how he got a girl pregnant."

My fingers curl up in the cold sand. I chew on my bottom lip until I draw blood. Why did he tell someone? "I see."

Scott leans back on his hands and tries to read my expression. "You okay?"

I nod. "Yeah I guess so." Clearly, I wasn't.

"Hey, you wanna come to a kickback later? My house. V and Dan can come, too," he asks, his body a little closer to mine.

I scoot over just an inch. He notices, but doesn't say anything.

"Uhm, maybe," I say.

"Okay. Just, uh—let me know."

He turns around and digs through a blue beach bag we brought. He takes out a fruit bowl of strawberries and mangoes.

"Want some?" he offers with a smile, a smile that feels even brighter and warmer than the sun.

"Sure."

We pick up the fruit with our fingers, and the mango and strawberry are so ripe that the sweet juice melts on my tongue. The sugar dissolves and quenches my body with a sweetness that I didn't know I needed.

Scott grabs a piece of strawberry and throws it up in the air. He tries to catch it in his mouth but it bonks off his nose.

"Haha, whatta fail," I say, and the laughter rising from my chest comes out in raw, untuned notes, as if my body was trying to remember how to laugh again.

"Okay okay, I'll get this one," he insists. He throws up a clump of mango and it lands in his mouth, though juice splats around his face. I giggle, he laughs, and we are covered in mango and strawberry and sunset, and for the first time in a while, I believe that I can be happy again.

Chapter 18: Grey Cotton Clouds

Don' need a girl right now sometimes

heartbreak serves a purpose to save—

- MAX.

Scott texted Max that same day, when he sat with Nura at the beach and decided to have a kickback.

Hey im having people over at my

place tonight

You coming?

Max striped down his black work attire and slipped on a t-shirt and shorts before he read the text and replied:

Yaaa

ill bring some drinks

He'd been working since eleven that morning, but it felt he'd been working for fuckin' days.

It was only eight, so he had some time to chill before going. He already had a couple of bottles of vodka, so he didn't have to go to the store.

He sat on his grey bed, then turned on some music—soft beats against the cloud of speakers. With the bong already in his hand, he cut up the weed to put in the bowl and grabbed a black lighter. The flame flicked onto the herb and white clouds spun at the bottom as he inhaled until he couldn't anymore. He blew out a stream of smoke, thick like cotton but with a hint of a cloudy grey against his grey blanket walls.

His head buzzed just slightly as he fell onto his bed and closed his eyes.

She was sad. When he told her that he didn't want to be with her. Big brown eyes shining with tears in the sunlight glow—it was hard to not feel bad.

He knew that. He knew he would break her heart, but she was better off. She'd heal. She didn't have the baby, at least. He'd be a crappy father. But for some reason, he kept turning over the middle of the night, reaching for her and thinking she was there.

He would tap on empty spaces like drums. Always, she would not be there, and he would feel a slight drop in his chest. Disappointment? Maybe relief, actually.

He took another hit from the bong.

It's only been a week, really. Surely he'd get over it soon enough. He'd just get onto some other girl at Scott's party or something. Easy enough.

Ding. The message on his phone screen blared at him.

Scott:

see ya there

Chapter 19: Pink Ambrosia

Clear pink drink
in a glass
sweet burn
down my throat
sways me in heaven
until I remember
maybe it's not ambrosia
but the answers
to my amnesia

- Nura Hart

V and I drank the Pink Ambrosia, well, that's what I call it, because the burn of the vodka soothed me somehow but the sweet fruit—like raspberries, and maybe strawberry and peach—sugared the burn.

Scott just took a beer, and about ten other people were there with some sort of drink in their hands. Dan didn't want to come because he had to get up early for work at the car shop, but I begged V to come with, and of course she came.

It was only ten minutes into the "kickback" when I suspected that, as the knocks on the door kept coming, this would be a little bigger than some kickback.

I got an uneasy feeling about this.

But of course, I know what that reason was.

Because the last time I was at an out-of-control drunken college party, I woke up with my virginity gone. Unwillingly. Without knowing who it was, ever. And I didn't think to go to the police, because how could they find out who it was? DNA, if even that? Plus, everyone would find out somehow. The drunken girl who cried rape. Uhg.

Stop thinking about this, Nura.

I take another gulp of my drink and keep drinking until the glass is empty. I instantly feel the alcohol float to my head and wobble to my toes. And it feels great.

"Whoaa, might wanna slow down there," Scott says, walking over and putting a hand on my shoulder; blush rushes up to my cheeks, but I use my hair as a curtain to keep him from noticing.

"Eh, it's okay, I don't really drink much anymore so it'll probably be my only drink of the night," I say. Scott flashes a smile, and for some reason I think about that night again. The damned night. Was he there, maybe? No, I'm just getting a little buzzed. I should just sit down. I walk over to the living room, grabbing V's arm, and plop us on the soft, dark blue cushions of the corner sofa.

"You good fam?" V laughs as I sigh and close my eyes.

"Yeahh. . . just, I, dunno. Haven't drank in a while, I guess."

She giggles and pats my shoulder. “No worries. I’ll be right here.”

I jump up at the sound of the door opening and a voice that could not be mistaken.

“Scott!” I dare to turn around. And there he is. Max. He’s holding beers and a single red rose—fuck, he’s with another girl here, isn’t he? One of the thorns of the rose stabs my chest.

“Oh shit,” V curses under her breath. We turn around before he can catch my face. I hear a crowd of voices flood into the house, and Max’s voice is lost in the sounds.

“I need a drink.” I get up off the couch, totally sober now, and fix myself up another Pink Ambrosia. V follows. I take a sip, then a gulp, then another gulp and gulp and gulp until the drink is gone.

“Ohhkayy, I think that’s enough for you,” V says, taking my empty glass. My blood warms and paints my cheeks pink.

"What is he even doing here?" I remember Scott saying that he was at Planned Parenthood for Max. So he must be good friends with him. He must've invited him. But why wouldn't he tell me that before? Because he's a jackass wanting to show that he's going to fuck his best friend's
ex-girlfriend? Or maybe he wants us to fix things because Max asked him to invite me? Neither made sense.

"Well. He's clearly friends with Scott. We can go if you want," V offers.

"No, I was here first. He can leave if he wants to." Music pumps through Scott's speakers. The bright lights in the living room go off and neon circles take over. I grin. "I'm going to have *fun*."

"You sure?"

"Absolutely." We link arms and walk into the crowd of people holding solo cups and moving their bodies with the music. I dove in with V behind me and let the music wave through my hips.

The alcohol hits me right then.

And I let go of myself. I dance and don't give a fuck how ridiculous I look, and I don't care if my shorts are riding up my ass or if I look bloated—I'm fine and free. I get lost in blackness.

Someone brushes their hand against my waist and I freeze. I don't know why, but I'm alarmed. The cold hand falls down toward my ass, but then the touch leaves me and holds my hand instead.

I turn around and he's there, staring at me with one corner of his lip turned up, but his eyes are a sad, mourning ocean—or an intoxicated ocean. I shake my head and start to leave, but he takes my wrist and tries to lead me out of the crowd.

"Don't!" I shout, though the music mutes me. I'm helpless and no one seems to notice.

The flashing neon lights bring me back to that darkness. Max looks at me as I dance. I'm suffocating with heavy breaths and the memories flood back, little by little, and I'm drowning in his eyes and I can't figure out what's real and what's in the past and what's here. Max pulls me and then I'm back in that darkness and I'm going into that dark room and the he throws me onto the bed and I want to *scream.*

"Nura! Nura!" I hear V cry. She's shaking my shoulders and the darkness slips away.

I break back into the reality. In a plain bedroom with a queen bed and a nightstand—quiet, the walls softening the music and people. Max stands behind her with an unreadable expression on his face.

"Nura?" he says.

“Get the hell outta here,” V orders, her voice hissing like a violent cat.

“What happened?” I ask.

“You were crying on the dance floor, Nura,” Max answered.

“She didn’t ask you,” V snaps.

“It’s okay, V . . .” I put a hand on her shoulder. “I’m sorry.”

“Don’t be.”

I jump as the door swings open. Scott barges in, his eyebrows knit together with concern. “Everything okay?” He asks. My cheeks are probably damp and red from crying so I wipe my face with my hand.

I nod. “Yeah, it’s fine. I just need to take a break.”

“Can I talk to you, Nura? Alone?” Max asks, looking between Scott and Nura. I swear I see him glare at Scott, but it was too fast for me to really know if he did. V raises her eyebrows at me, asking if I’m okay with that. I nod. Scott sighs and glares back at Max—I didn’t mistake that for sure.

V and Scott leave, still looking at me in case I change my mind. But I don’t. They close the door, but I suspect that V will stay outside the door to make sure I’m okay.

We’re alone.

I look down so his eyes won’t draw me in. I hear him walk closer, cautiously, to make sure I’m okay with it. He sits down on the queen bed of white sheets. The blanket is cold and a little stiff, as it hasn’t been slept in for years.

The Pink Ambrosia’s effects quickly die down as he takes my hand. My heart drums up my blood to a pleasant boil. I miss him.

"Nura. . . I'm sorry. For everything."

There it is. The words I've wanted him to say to me. I fight back the tears and slip my hand away from his.

Chapter 20: Red Rose

I said I don' need a girl but she stayed in my head and now I'm here with a fuckin' red rose she never really left baby save me from this cold. . .

- MAX.

I've been avoiding getting too deep in my music. And the story.

I don't want to get too close to it because it still hurts sometimes to think about, but I realize now that hiding behind third person isn't going to help. I didn't even know what the fuck third person meant until I met Nura an' she told me I should try third or second person in one of my songs an' I tried them out an' . . .

So yeah, this is me. The real me.

That night of Scott's party, I remembered that she loved roses.

I don't know why, but when I was at the store buying beers, I saw a dozen, took one and left. I forgot about it until Scott opened the door to his place.

"Had a hot date or somethin' bro?" Scott teased, pointing at the rose still in my hand.

"Oh, nah. I just had it and well, chicks love roses."

Scott grinned and pat my back. "Alright, man."

I stepped inside and could've sworn I saw a swish of long, dark brown hair in the kitchen. *Nura*, I thought. But there were a lot of girls with dark brown hair. What did I really care, anyway? She was kinda crazy and got too attached to me. I didn't need to care anymore. We were over.

I broke the long stem of the rose and stuffed it into my pocket. I set the beers down and helped Scott out with the music.

"Oh hey, by the way, your ex is here," Scott said.

I snapped my head toward him. "What? Why?"

He shrugged, as if it wasn't a big deal. "I invited her."

"What the hell, man?"

He smiles. "Yo, look man, she's friends with my friend, and she seems cool. There's gonna be a lot of people, so you probably won't even see her."

"You suck," I joked and pushed him, a little pissed, but Scott was my homie. I'd be cool.

We cranked up the music and people flooded in the living room from the kitchen. I cracked open a beer with Scott. He turned off main lights and turned on the neon ones.

"Cheers," he said, lifting up his beer bottle. His teeth flashed in pink and green. He looked kinda . . . strange like that. Evil. But I was tripping. I did kinda smoke a lot before I got there.

I shook my head and just drank. Some girl bumped against me and apologized with a flirty smile. She had long blonde hair and a tight red shirt that made her D cups pop out, so I chugged my beer and followed her into the crowd of people.

She asked my name, and I yelled it, and she yelled back her name—I think it was Hannah or Anna, maybe Savannah. She smirked and turned around and grinded against me—a sure thing. I put my hands on her waist and wanted to ask her to go somewhere private, but just as I leaned in her neck to kiss her and ask—I saw *her*.

She was dancing in front of me, but her back was turned. Scott stood behind her, reaching for her. I got strange Deja vu, like I'd seen this before. Scott and Nura had never been at the same party before, at least not with me. Scott put a hand on her waist and I caught her reaction immediately: her shoulders tensed. Her dancing slowed. *Was he trying to––nah, he wouldn't.*

But his hand moved down toward her ass.

That fucking bastard.

I shoved the girl grinding on me to the side and yanked Scott off of Nura.

"What the hell, man?" I shouted.

"The fuck's wrong with you?" Scott yelled, pushing me backward. I swayed back but kept my balance. A few people stopped dancing to stare. I chuckled.

"Max—" Nura cried, her wide brown eyes glimmered with tears. I couldn't stand it. Her chest moved up and down, panicking. I didn't know what else to do, so I pulled her away but she yelled and knocked my hand off hers and sobbed.

I glared at Scott. "Stay away from her." He did something to upset her, he must have. I took Nura by the hand again and cut through the dancing bodies. She didn't fight back this time.

But her friend V came over and told me to let her go. "Get her to a room!" I yelled. I let V take her, but I still followed them to make sure she'd do what I told her.

Why the hell am I doing this? I asked myself. Why did I still feel responsible for her even though we were over?

I had a perfectly hot girl ready to jump on me, but instead I was wasting my time on a broken girl that I ditched a week ago. I almost turned back around once we got into a room, but when I saw V shake Nura, I asked if she was okay. V just told at me to get the hell out.

I figured she would know Nura better than me, so I stepped toward the door, but Scott barged in.

A fire scorched through me. There was no way in hell I would leave her now.

"Everything okay?" Scott asked.

I wanted to punch him. But Nura responded to him in her small, kind voice. Her eyes warmed up at his concern and I remembered when she looked at me that way before. *Fuck, why do I feel like screaming right now?*

"Can I talk to you, Nura? Alone?" I blurted out, staring straight into her eyes. V and Scott looked at Nura for an answer.

She nodded, and my chest fell in relief. Scott and V passed a stare at me as they closed the door, but I sat on the bed and stared Scott down right back and the son of a bitch smirked.

She looked down at her hands and picked at her nails. She always did that when she was nervous or wanted to hide. She didn't want anyone to discover her, but she used to want me to. And I didn't care to. *What the fuck's wrong with me?*

I wrapped my hand around her small hand. She was cold instead of her usual warmth.

"Nura. . . I'm sorry. For everything."

She slipped her hand away from mine. Took a deep breath.

"Sure," she said, turning her head away from me. She didn't believe me. Couldn't really blame her for that.

The red rose poked around in my pocket. It was probably all crumpled up, but I took it out anyway. The petals were a little crushed, but still whole. I offered it to her, and her whole body gravitated toward the flower, even her tears seemed to move toward it.

She looked into my eyes, a loving look that I crushed before. Her cheeks were as red as the petals on the flower, and just as soft as them, too. I couldn't forget that feeling.

Her fingers curled around the rose and I let go of it. She held it to her nose and took a deep breath, closing her eyes. Her damp eyelashes brushed against her cheeks. Her lips curved just slightly, and that was enough for me. To just see even a little bit of her happiness.

"I think about you all the time," I said, an over-exaggeration that I hoped would win her over.

She opened her eyes. "Thank you," she said, "But I can't do this again."

And she placed the red rose down on the bed. It bled its petals on the white sheets.

Chapter 21: Jagged Lines

A soft wave
to float along with you
only to find
that you had a storm
in your eyes
and the jagged lines
of lighting
electrified me
and cut me
and left me
weaker than ever

- *Nura Hart*

When Max got more and more flakey, and I held in my anger because he said he loved me, I got desperate for answers. So by early August, I looked up psychics.

I'd never been to a psychic before, but I just wanted to try it and see if it would make any sense of this.

I looked up Yelp reviews and found one that seemed kinda legit. Her name was Suki, and she was a life coach *and* a psychic, so either way I would get some useful advice, right? I made an appointment online, and the site said that bringing pictures always helped. So I pulled up some pictures of Max to bring

The next day, just a couple of weeks before we broke up, I drove to the address, expecting to see some random building in a row of a shopping complex, but instead I drove up to a large, pale yellow house with a koi pond in the front yard. The green grass and leafy bushes brushed against the wind; it was as if I was about to enter into a place of magic.

I knocked twice on the white door. After a mere two seconds, the door opened. An older lady with short, dirty blonde hair with grey strands, dark pink lipstick, and a pink shirt and long pants greeted me. She looked *normal*—nothing like I'd imagine. No long, over-jeweled wrists, no oversized poncho with Indian designs or weird fortune teller spheres around.

"Hello dear, just give me two minutes to prepare! Come, sit," her voice was soft and soothing with a slight accent that I couldn't decipher exactly, but it was comforting. She led me to an open room, the walls covered with bookshelves, all filled up with books. My heart leaped at the sight; I wanted a room just like that someday. I still do.

I waited, a little nervous. What would she say? What if she saw everything, including the darkness inside my past? Worse, what if she saw the darkness in Max, the darkness that I already suspected was there?

I didn't want to have to let him go, though my instincts told me I should.

Suki came back into the room and clapped her hands. "Alright, let's go dear!" She led me upstairs to a room with two, grand wooden chairs decorated with red cushions. More books and stones and statues of what looked like goddesses and gods stacked on the shelf across from the chairs.

"Okay. . .so, I will get started with some meditation. So you can clear your mind."

I nodded. She sat down on one chair and I sat on the other just beside her.

"Breathe in. Deep breathe, and close your eyes," she told me. So I did. I kept breathing. I imagined an ocean, a beach, sand that I could sink my feet into as the cool saltwater blanketed over them and soaked into my skin with the sun. Breathe.

My shoulders fell and muscles melted into complete relaxation. I could feel her smiling. “Okay, open your eyes, dear.”

But once I did, my shoulders tensed again.

She asked me what I wanted to ask, and I told her that there was this man, and I didn’t know how he felt for me exactly or what I should do with him. Should I stay, should I go—what?

“Do you have a picture?” she asked. I did, so I gave her the picture. It was of us, on a random, drunken night in his room. A little selfie with my arms wrapped around his neck. I was a smiling fool.

She studied it.

"Hmm. . .He's very bright, gifted. . . but, but there is a sort of unsteadiness about him. Uhm, but I feel dat, what I mean with unsteadiness is dat, uhm, he feels like he's subject to a lot of fluctuations of mood, of, uhm, showing affection one day but not the next days. A lot of ups and downs in his energy field, yes?"

Goosebumps formed on my arm—*did it just colder in here?*

"He's not the most stabilizing energy for you, my dear," she smiled as if to say, "you know this." I nodded. Because I did know this. I just hoped maybe someone would tell me that I was just overthinking it.

She raised her eyebrows then went on. "Mmmm. . . Uhm. . . I—I like his intensity, mmmmm, but I also feel he can drift off into negativity, to where nothing is right, to where he sort of poo poos everything dat's good," she laughed and I laughed with her, appreciating her effort to make this a little less serious. "And he can get into a real downward spiral before you know it, he's just like urggghh." She made a fist that almost exactly described my reactions to his instability with me.

"How long have you known him?"

"Uhm . . . almost three months now, I think." *Was it sad that I didn't bother to keep track like most couples would?*

She paused for what seemed like a long minute.

"It seems, well, you are a wave of gently ups and downs." She made a motion with her arm of smooth ocean waves.

"You have experienced much *much* tragedy and pain, but you still are smoother waves."

I thought about my parents then. How my father drank, and how my mother was lonely because of it, but still stayed with him because sometimes they would sneak around and kiss in the kitchen in the evenings when they thought I had gone to bed. But they were both gone now because of his drinking.

Tears welled up in my eyes. I breathe to hold them back.

"Him, when he is up, he brings you way up, up beyond the sky." I laugh and nod because he did make me feel that way: when he kissed me, when he slept next to me, when I heard his deep, smoky voice slip through the air and fill my ears with a music that I could dance or fall asleep or just live in.

Suki sighed, though, frowning. "But, when he is down, he brings you *down*." She motioned her arm to the ground. "He has jagged lines. And dat's no good, dear. He does care, but his addictions make it so he cannot care dat much."

I froze, syncing in the reality that I knew already.

"You care for him," she said.

I nodded.

"You should communicate dat. If you cannot, he is not the one for you, dear."

I knew she was right. But I also think I knew that if I told him how much I really cared, he wouldn't want to hear it, which meant that he wasn't right for me, which meant that I would have to leave him at one point. Or he would leave me.

He would leave me, I knew it. Because I didn't have the strength to break it off. I couldn't help it—I loved him.

So I left Suki's house with a dread, heavy in my heart, a dread that told me that things with Max would end soon.

His jagged lines would cut me into pieces.

Chapter 22: Grey Cotton Clouds pt. 2

Grey cotton clouds
clog my soul
with cold rain

- *Nura Hart*

I leave him in the room with the crumpled rose he tried to give me, thinking *he's never given anything to me before, except a lunch here and there*. So why now? Why, when he could've been this nice while we were actually together?

It's too late. I won't go back to him. Besides, he doesn't really want to be with me. He just wants to fuck me again.

V isn't outside the room like I thought she would be—I guess she decided it was okay to give us privacy after all—but she stood at the end of the hall, as if she was a wall between the party and the quiet space, and was ready for me to fall into her arms and cry.

Sometimes missing him gets so overwhelming that tears fog my eyes. And if I'm alone, I let them sit until they turn into a waterfall. If I'm around people, or about to see people, I breathe and blink and bury them back into my body, but I can't hold them for much longer.

She wraps an arm around me as we weave through the crowd. Air saturated with sweat and heat clings onto my skin and tears. "Is she okay?"

I peek up and see that it's Scott.

His butterscotch eyes strike me so suddenly in the darkness that I can't tell if I'm drawn towards them or afraid of them. He places his calloused hand on my shoulder, filled with prickling warmth that soothes the aches I didn't know I had, and leads me out the door with V.

Once we get to the door and fall into the cool night, I can breathe again. The sounds of the party scatter in whispers in the night.

V charges ahead to the car, but Scott stops me on the lawn. He doesn't say anything. He just smooths his fingers against my arms. I suck in a load of air and tense up.

"What is it, Scott?"

He looks into my eyes and the corner of his lips curve up. "I'm sorry," he whispers.

I furrow my eyebrows and shake my head in confusion. "For what?"

"Max." His fingers move to my cheeks, where tears have fallen, and I close my eyes to purge them out. I don't want to cry about Max anymore.

"It's not your fault."

His Adam's apple moves up and down as he purses his lips and leans toward me. I don't stop him.

He presses his lips against mine and he's consuming me and I am burning alive; the feeling surges through me and I don't know if I like his kiss or if I like the distraction of feeling something other than the heartache from a boy who has hurt me over and over and over again.

"Hey!" V shouts. I turn and she's waving her hand out. "C'mon Nura!"

I break away from Scott, my cheeks sticky. I feel sick, so I whip around and don't look back at Scott as I walk to the car.

V doesn't say anything until we've been on the road for a few miles.

"Uhm. . . you don't have to tell me if you don't want to, but what happened with Max? And why did Scott kiss you?"

I shake my head. "Nothing really. I think Max wants to be together again, but. . . I said I can't do it anymore."

"Good. He doesn't deserve you, Nura." She holds my hand.

"And Scott?"

I shake my head. "You know about as much as I do."

She sighs and says, "Dear Lord, girl," then squeezes my hand, and I know that V will always be my best friend.

We get to our apartment and I walk straight to my room after saying goodnight. I don't even bother to change. I just fall onto my bed, a colossal pile of grey and purple blankets, and stare at my window.

The clouds cover the moon, fluffy and grey. Grey cotton clouds. No stars, no moon, no light. I wonder if he really misses me. I wonder if his words that claimed he thinks about me all the time are true.

Max, come back. . . I want to come back. . . GOD, Nura. You're pathetic. Just shut the fuck up and get on with your love life for crying out loud! It's not like you don't have options!

Rolling my eyes at myself

Wow, you really are insane aren't you, Nura?

Maybe, maybe.

My thoughts race and I can't sleep, so I grab a piece of paper and a pen, then sit at my desk to write a letter that I will never send.

Max,

I don't want to admit that I loved you. I never wanted to admit it, even to myself. But now I've accepted it and it's killing me because I miss you and I can't tell you because it's not like you'd be able to do anything about it. And it's not like you ever felt the same way. I know you didn't, and I know you never will.

There are times when I just curl up in my bed, alone. With you, it's always the perfect temperature; warm, just warm, because when I feel too hot, you cool me, and when I'm cold, you are warm.
So I bury myself in the pillows and comforter and blankets that are apart from you and do not amount to what your body provided for me. Even if we didn't sleep skin to skin, your presence, your body next to mine, just arm length's away, was all I needed.

But you didn't want to be with me anymore. Because you don't need a girl. Because you didn't take me seriously.

I think I left the pieces of myself with you, and you scattered them away from you because you didn't want them anymore. Now I'm finding them, piece by piece. I'm just trying to figure out if I'm supposed to live the rest of my life without you in it or if you're supposed to be in my life. But I'm starting to think that I just don't want you in my life. You hurt me, and you will continue to. And I hurt you too, I think, or maybe not. But if I did, I'm sorry. Really. I'm moving on. I have to.

- *Nura*

Before stepping into the shower, I turn on a cover of "The Scientist" by Corianne. His old voicemails play in my head at the same time. It's like a sad, broken scene in a movie. I sit down and hold myself, my arms wrapped around my knees.

Hot floods of tears strike me and I gasp and sob because that empty hole inside me burns. My hair becomes a curtain around my face as the water soaks me. I imagine myself crying, naked, in the middle of a hot storm because that's what it feels like. It burns, a reminder that he is not here with me and that really, that's the best thing for me.

Stop missing someone who doesn't miss you.

Stop loving someone who doesn't love you.

I take a breath. Let my tears melt with the hot water flowing down my body.

I should like someone like Scott, right? Why didn't I?

He was obviously kinder and warmer and just happier—better for me. But I don't think about the kiss again when I see a missed call from him and a couple of texts.

Dammit.

I throw on clothes and slip out into the night.

Chapter 23: Rose Skin

Soft mountain curves
carved along your arms
that lead to a shoulder
of roses
I kissed them awake
hoping they would grow
toward me
and you gave me
your arm and shoulder
but never your hand.

- *Nura Hart*

The week after I saw the psychic, I got ready to see Max again. I put on a black skirt and crop top and sprayed my favorite rose perfume. I went to pick him up from his friend's house again.

He hopped into my car and kissed me, like always. He lay his hand on my thigh, leaned into me, like always. Then asked in his smoky voice, “Did you miss me?”

“Ha, noo,” I teased and pushed his face away from mine. I tried hard not to grin, but whenever I saw him and he touched me I burst with this excited, electric feeling. I didn’t want to admit that I’d been dying to see him just so I could prove the psychic wrong.

“C’mon, did you miss me?” He asked again, brushing his lips on my shoulder.

I shrugged. “Eh.”

He smiled and took his hand off my thigh. “Fineeee, I didn't really miss you either."

When we got to his house, we went to his room, and he asked, “How much did you miss me?”

I smiled and didn't say anything.

“Alrighttttt, fine you don't feel the same,” he joked, then inhaled a load of smoke from his vape.

I moved toward him at the edge of the bed and held his arm, feeling the ridges of muscle and traced the rose tattoo on his shoulder. “Noooo, I *did* miss you.” I bit down my bottom lip and played along, feeling heat between my legs and spreading up through my body. “Trust me,” I added.

His lips curved up. “Can I trust you?” he asked, eyebrows raised.

It caught me off guard. I didn’t expect him to really care whether he could trust me or not. But I liked the possibility that he did. “Of course you can,” I said, then traced the tattoo on his other shoulder, a treble clef. His muscles curved like they were part of a carved sculpture.

"Do you trust *me*?" He leaned his forehead on mine, then exhaled smoke, slowly, out from his lips to mine. A smoke kiss.

And of course, under that spell, I could respond with nothing other than: "Yeah, I do."

"So can I ask something?"

I closed my eyes, preparing myself for his question. "Sure."

"Why did you wanna have sex? With me? You know, I'm kinda fucked up." He slid his forehead away from mine and touched my neck with his lips—no, not a kiss, just a touch. Shivers tickled down my spine. I let out a sigh and held his face in my hands, leading his eyes to look into mine. His ocean crawled toward me, wanting me.

"Because. . ." I kissed him, then whispered, "Because you don't take Oxy."

We both burst into laughter and kissed again. "Mmm yeah I can't really afford more drugs," he said.

"Yeah, you might want to do a little less." I reached for his pants, but he stopped me.

"Don't tell me that." He glared at me. Scoffed. Shook his head. "Don't be like everyone else." He pushed my hands off him and grabbed his bong.

And just like that, one moment, we were soaring in the sky with the sunset, swimming in colors of pink and blue and gold, and the next, I was stuck in the dirt while he climbed on, ahead, above, away—away from me. Above me. On my knees. Left in coldness because he didn't want to be told what to do. I didn't even mean to upset him.

The ups and downs. The sharp, jagged lines that the psychic warned me about. When he brings you down, he brings you down. And despite all their warnings, I couldn't leave.

I was addicted. He abused drugs, and I abused a different sort of drug, one that, once it pierces your skin and streams through your blood and reaches your heart, you might not ever be able to rid of—Max.

"Sorry," I said, and as he smoked, I traced the rose on his left shoulder, skin soft but the muscle underneath hard and alive as he moved at my touch. The same way I moved when he rested his hand on my waist, curved into me to create an hourglass, muscles soft against my tan skin, more fluid against his touch.

"It's okay, baby." I inhaled and tried to control my exhales as he moved his hand down and forgave me.

Max's skin betrayed me; soft and smooth, even with the tattoos, but his muscles had told me the truth: he was a hard man, like the rock of a sculpture. Or just ice. Cold, hard.

And now I'm back on his bed for another fix of him. I trace his rose skin again and he kisses mine, soaked in that rose perfume and lotion. Somehow the scene is complete: he has the rose, I have the smell, and together there is life. Apart, there is just a rose. There is just a smell. One of the senses is always blinded.

So if I want to see the rose, I have to stay right here, with him.

Still, I leave in the morning while he sleeps, because the bright morning seeping in through the cracks of the door sobers me awake and I remember that the cycle will start all over again.

The rose he tried to give me on the party is crumpled on his night stand. I leave that too.

Chapter 24: Grey Waves

She told me once I should stop with the drugs and I didn't listen and now she's gone but the drugs are still stashed in my cabinets—what do I really need her for?

- *MAX.*

I fell onto my bed, grey sheets crumbled up. The alcohol still buzzed through me. I reached my hand out, tapping on empty spaces like drums.

I turned my head to the space:

A lifeless puddle of sheets.

I reached for my phone on the grey-carpeted floor next to my bed and scrolled through my phone history. I *did* call her last night after she left the party. But she didn't answer the first time. Did she come over?

Are *we* over?

Fuck, what time is it?

The bright numbers on my phone screamed: 7:00am. I still had some hours before work. So I threw my phone back on the ground and rolled over on my stomach, falling into blackness and dreams of her, of sand pulling into waves clouded with a sunless grey and those waves crashing onto the sand—kissing and destroying.

Scott texted me later and asked me if I was "cool."

I dunno if I was. Maybe a little hungover. But I felt weird for some reason. What happened last night exactly?

I had seen Nura at Scott's party—she was dancing.

A messed-up rose was on my nightstand. Right. I gave it to her. Or tried to.

She looked really wasted. *Really* wasted.

Neon lights flashed across her face. And Scott. She danced with Scott, and she was letting him touch her? But then I danced with her. I felt her against my body and she was happy and charming and smiling with her glowing makeup and wavy hair. But then, why was she dancing with Scott too?

But when Scott touched her, she freaked out. V and I took her to a room. Scott came in.

I talked to her. She left. I followed, but she didn't see me.

I watched her go out the door with Scott's hand on her shoulder and my chest got hot and my hands fell to my sides. And out the window, I saw Scott kiss her. She kissed him back. And I crushed the rose in my fist.

That was what happened. *Right*? I shook my head. I needed some water. So I went upstairs and texted Scott back:

Idkkk dont remember much ha

'Cept you kissed my girlfriend you dick.

I gulped down a glass of water and set it down on the counter.

But she's not my girlfriend.

A half-empty bottle of grey goose sat on the counter.

I got a weird Deja vu feeling in the pit of my stomach. I went back downstairs and smoked a bowl before getting in the shower, hoping to wash away the weird vibes. But I couldn't stop thinking about last night.

She came over. We had sex. So it must've been her and I dancing last night? Why did I see Scott then? Ah, a dream. Ha. He just kissed her, and it was probably because he was so drunk. *I* was out of it too.

I grinned as I got out of the shower because we aren't over after all. It was great. We would fuck again and it'd be cool.

I would just be more careful this time.

The red rose on my nightstand was turning grey, so I threw it out. She didn't want it anyway.

Chapter 25: Sun Kissed

Rays hug my skin
like a long lost
best friend that tickles
my cheeks and lungs
and holds my body
when cold
You,
You.
A gold light
and healthy kiss—
my sun kiss

- *Nura Hart*

Tap tap tap.

The soft warmth of my heater feathers over to me and sways my window curtains as I wake to a knock on my door. A single stream of sunlight peers at me.

"Hey, sorry if I woke you," Scott's voice cushions the sharp pierce of confusion I feel after getting back from Max's house. I sit up on my bed and manage a smile.

"Oh no, it's okay. I wasn't sleeping. What's up?"

"You up for the beach?" Scott flashes his bright, irresistible smile. I sigh and manage a laugh. Why not? Anything to get my mind off of last night.

"Sure," I say.

At the beach, I feel strangely bare with just my bikini in front of Scott, and I don't know why, but the sun warms me, enough to feel a little better. Though I left Max as soon as the sun rose. I didn't want to wake up again and hope that maybe he'd change again.

No, I need to start new.

"What are the odds you run in with me?" Scott asks.

I shiver at the thought of hopping into the cold water, but Scott holds my hand, his skin still filled with the end-of-August heat. The white clouds, the light, the warmth—us. I should have realized I just wanted someone to push away the clouds when they got too overwhelming for me to shine, to smile. Even though it felt weird last night, I want to have fun and not think about it. Plus, I need to rinse away the stickiness of leftover alcohol and sweat on my skin.

I bite down on my bottom lip. "Hmm . . . One in three."

"Alright." Scott shrugs and starts counting. "Three. . . two. . .one. . ."

"Two."

"Two."

We laugh. "Oh god. Okay." I squeal as I stripped off my flip flops and take a deep breath.

"You ready?" He asks. I nod. He squeezes my hand, and the bright sunlight surges through me. And it feels tingly and different.

It's just fun, though. I deserve fun, so I start to run, breaking his hand from mine, running

and running

running—

I crash into the waves. He laughs and his smile glows in the sun. And I'm swimming against the waves, against my darkness, my struggles, my past—everything.

I'm going so far into the ocean and I don't care because I'm fighting back, and I'm going to go far because I can survive. I know I will.

And I have to remember, I think. I have to remember what happened that night. I dive in deep, deep in the deep waters. The unknown.

I think of Max as the waves course through me and with me and all around me. And soon, I find that I am too far in and the currents are too strong—they're pulling me further and further into the unknown and I try to pull myself up from the water, but it's spinning and pushing me down and flipping my hair in my face and I want to cough out the salt scratching my throat but I have no air and it's dark and there's Max it's dark neon lights and his blue eyes glow and he smiles I love him I love him but I'm falling into that darkness I love him—

And I'm drowned black blood.

Chapter 26: Purple Denial

Curled in the soft clouds
of my purple blanket
oceans gush
from my eyes
and turn my lips
purple,
oceans,
absent of him

and sun rays
peak at me but
I want to hold on
to my purple blanket,
to warm
my dying, purple lips.

- *Nura Hart*

I shiver in my big white sweater, even though I took a hot shower for so long that my fingers wrinkled and the mirror fogged up. At the beach, Scott paddled in with his surfboard to save me and the rest is kind of a blur. I was so cold that my lips are still a dark purple, like death.

We were in his black BMW when Scott asked me why I went so far, his voice soft and sad. My hair dripped, and he had wrapped me in a towel, but sand stuck in-between my toes and fingers and scratched my body.

I didn't answer until we got to my apartment. "I was trying to find something."

"Find what?" he asked.

I shook my head. He didn't say more as he walked me up my apartment.

He's been talking to V for a little bit now. She just got back from her lunch with Dan. I don't know what he's told her, but at this point, I don't care. I just want to be warm.

Ding.

My phone vibrates on my nightstand. I look, and my heart leaps.

Max. He asks if I'm okay. Did Scott tell him I almost drowned? Or did he know about the kiss? Scott wouldn't have told him about that, would he?

He texts again:

Why'd you leave so early?

A minute later:

I still think about you all the time

I think about you, too. But I know my thoughts are different than his. I know that my thoughts always become a physical ache. It spreads to my chest and stomach and squeezes my lungs until I can't breathe because I don't think I can breathe knowing that I, well, that *he*, will never love me.

That he will never miss me. That I will not be an everyday thought, but a passing thought, a casual breeze that comes and goes like the tick of a second.

I had never realized how much I liked being around him until I was no longer, or could no longer, be around him.

I'm exhausted and know I shouldn't reply to him, so I shut my curtains and turn off my lights. I let it all fade into darkness as I curl into my purple blanket and cry out, "Please make it stop *please*. . ." I don't know who I'm asking, but I'm desperate for answers.

My fists and sobs choke that blanket, and I think I may be going a little crazy.

Because I start to smell the vanilla—vanilla smoke.

Do I even deserve better? Am I forever cursed to care for others and be there for them and never have anyone to fall back on? God, I'm pathetic. Nura, get a fucking grip on yourself!

I close my eyes and breath. I imagine him lying next to me; his muscles curving next to mine.

Then I see that body smoking into the air, leaving me, and I can't do anything about it.

I remember telling him about that night. The night I've tried so hard to forget.

I had picked him up from the bar around midnight—nothing new. It was toward the end of our relationship, when things began to go a little downhill. He'd gotten sick, I ignored him, he called me, we made up, I got pregnant, etc., etc. Right before.

He slumped into the car, the night streets trickling with people going back home in Ubers and Lyfts or just walking to wherever their feet could take them.

"Thanks babe," he said and leaned in for a kiss. I smirked and kissed him, giving me a little shiver up my spine.

I got onto the freeway, heading to his house.

"I feel kinda anxious sometimes." He spoke to the window, so I didn't know if he wanted me to respond. Still, it made me curious. This was the second time that he had suddenly decided to open up conversation about serious things. Things I always wanted to know.

"Why?" I asked.

He shrugged. "I dunno. Been like that since I was a kid."

I nodded. I still didn't know what to say. I thought maybe he just wanted me to listen. "I'm sorry, Max."

He breathed and leaned his head back on the seat, then chuckled. "Was I really your first?"

I knew what he meant. I stayed silent for a minute, staring at the long stretch of freeway, only a few other cars on the road alongside us. There weren't any stars out. A rare summer night of clouds.

"No," I whispered, but before he could respond, I added, "I don't really remember my first time."

His eyes burned with blue fire on me, but I kept my eyes on the road because I couldn't even look at him as I thought about it. I wanted to erase the memories I did have. It was pointless to remember anyway.

He seemed to understand what I meant and put his hand on my thigh. “Do you know who it was?”

I shook my head. “No. It was too dark, and I was too drunk. A Labor Day weekend party.”

He didn’t react to it really. He was just silent.

Darkness and neon lights flash before me and dancing bodies circle around me. Black blood. And in my memory, I see him sometimes.

Like he was there, Max was there at the party. That night. That I was. . . raped. He’s in that memory, clear as day. But how could I forget seeing those eyes, so blue like the ocean that it seemed he was a part of it? I think I danced with him, but I’m not sure.

And I don’t want it to be true. Because I know if it’s true, then there’s one horrifying truth that I don’t think I would want to know.

No, it can’t be.

I open my eyes and stop trying to dream myself into thinking up my own nightmare.

Instead, I see the reality: a roomful of my life so far; the ocean art, the black-ink drawings of sad words and broken-hearted girls—me, the poetry, the maps from places I have yet to travel, and the pictures of the people that have made my life happy at one point or another. I open my eyes to this room and I see a girl who has lived so much life, but also has so much more to live.

There's still time to find happiness. There has to be.

I hold my phone and stare at the text from Max. I give in and type my reply, my thumbs shaking as I press each letter.

Have you met me before?

Chapter 27: Smoke Burns

This girl's making me crazy when I see him touch her fire burns my lungs and I'll smoke a whole bowl in one breath 'cause of her—

- MAX.

I sat on my bed with a pair of basketball shorts on and shook a towel through my wet shower hair. I didn't bother putting a shirt on 'cause it was too damn hot in there.

And I stared at Nura's text:

Have you met me before?

Is that supposed to be a trick question?

I texted her back:

What do ya mean?

Scott stumbled into my house, wagging his wet hair like a dog. My front door had been open, and since we were best friends, I never minded him barging in before.

I tried to not glare at him, but he was just at the beach with her. I saw them when I went to go surf by myself earlier. I thought Nura and I were good, but he kissed her at the party and hadn't said anything yet *and* went to the beach with her almost right after her and I slept together.

She went head into the ocean, going way too far into the tide. While Scott tried to look for her in the ocean like an idiot, swimming aimlessly, I surfed out for her, but Scott got to her before me.

I was thankful, but what the fuck was he thinking? Maybe it was 'cause he *was* my best friend, or maybe I didn't like seeing her with someone else at all. *Fuck, what's this chick doin' to me? Get on some other one already.*

"You good dude?" he asked.

"Yea, whatever," I said, looking back on my phone for Nura's response.

Had you met me before the bar?

Why would she think that? I flipped through my memory. I'd been confused earlier. . .thinking that maybe we had met before the bar, but that was just 'cause of last night. I was mixing memories up again, like always after too much to drink or smoking or both. *Man, maybe I need to stop for a while.*

I text Nura back quickly before I forget.

No, we met at the bar bb

Scott shrugged his backpack off and opened it up, a wet towel and took out a green canister.

"Didn't see you out there today. The waves were gnarly," he said, then grabbed my bong and packed up a bowl.

This was normal routine. Homies just hanging out and smokin', but now he was just pissing all over my personal space. *Dick.*

"I was out there," I said.

His skull-print lighter flickered on against his thumb as he steered the flame to the bowl and inhaled.

"What's up with you, man?" He passed the bong to me. I almost didn't take it, but I needed to at least smoke if I was gonna deal with this shit.

I sucked the air until my lungs burned. It didn't even phase me, the burn. I coughed my lungs out so I wouldn't have to say anything.

He nodded. "Lotta drama last night. Sorry 'bout that. Shouldn't have tried to intervene."

Instead of passing him the bong, I lay it down on the floor. "I know you're into her, man."

He stared at me, not smiling or frowning. I cleared my throat and stared right back. He smirked, breaking eye contact, and shrugged. "Why would you think that?"

He grabbed the bong off the floor. I didn't break my eye contact. "'Cause I saw you kiss her at the party."

Scott blew out smoke, coughed, and chuckled. "Yeaaah, I'm sorry 'bout that man. But it was a long time ago." He pat me on the back. "I was kinda drunk and she was hot and well, she kissed me back." He grinned.

"It wasn't that long ago. It was *last night.*"

Scott's grin faded. "Oh."

"Did you fuckin' kiss her before that too?" My chest flamed up like it did last night, and my body reacted—I swung my fist right at him, crushing the butterscotch glaze in his eyes.

Black blood gushed from his nose.

Chapter 28: Roses and Strawberries and Cigarettes

Smoky flower perfume
soaks in my skin
as I breathe in the cigarette
until it burns to death
and cover the smell
with petals of roses
and sugar of strawberries
But the smoke
Has seeped inside me.

- *Nura Hart*

I buy a pack of Spirits, light blue, and walk to an area by the beach closest to my apartment. I light up a cigarette, and a strawberry pink paints the closing sky, making me believe that there's still something beautiful and sweet in this fucked up place.

I'd been sitting my bed almost all day, the stress getting to me. So I decided to come out here and stress-smoke—try to figure out what I remember about that night. . .

The music thumped against my chest in the claustrophobic nightmare. I couldn't move through the crowd without accidentally brushing someone's ass. But I was too drunk to care, and that buzz moved my hips—'round and 'round and 'round.

A hand wrapped around my waist—hands, long and cupped around my waist—

DA DA DUN, DA DA DA DA DA DA DUN DA DA

My phone blares out and I snap out of my memory.

It's Max. I let the song go on. . .

Da da da da dun da da da, da da da da da dun da da

Darling you've got to let me know Should I Stay or Should I Go?

I answer it.

"Hello?"

"Hey. Come over. Please." My hand shakes when I hear his croaky voice because I can hear the fear in his voice—something's wrong. Really wrong.

"Are you okay?"

He hangs up before I can get an answer.

I toss my cigarette on the ground and crush it with my foot, the ashes crumpled underneath. I debate whether I should go to him. Figure out what he wants.

Should I stay or should I go?

Come over. Please.

I run to my car.

I get to his front door and stand for a minute before knocking.

There's no answer. I turn the knob. *Creeeaaaaakkkk. . .*

My pulse throbs in my neck and chest and wrists and my teeth clench tight down and I prepare myself to see something horrible—a dead body maybe? Max, did he call because he was dying, overdosing, something cold and awful and terrifying—

I burst out a breath of relief when Max storms out from his room and stands in front of me, fine, healthy, no blood anywhere.

He doesn't say anything. His lips are pressed in a tight line and eyes are darker than I've ever seen them. A cold shiver crawls down my spine.

"Are you seeing him?" he asks, his smoky voice like ice.

I hesitate a moment too long, I know it, but still I play dumb. "Who?"

"You know who." He takes a step closer to me. I step back.

I take a deep breathe, and—

"So *what*? Why do you even care, Max? You *broke* my heart! And *now* you want me? What the *hell*?" I let myself raise my voice at him because I know that I'm right and there's no fucking way that he's going to blame me for any of it. Not anymore.

"But my best friend! And while we were *together*!" He shouts back, lifting his hand up and pointing to the door as if Scott was right outside.

I cross my arms and scoff. "Uhm, I'm sorry, should I refresh your memory a little? YOU BROKE UP WITH ME. WE AREN'T TOGETHER!"

"WE WERE THOUGH! BACK THEN, WE WERE! HE TOLD ME!" He yells louder than I've ever heard him yell. Actually, he's never yelled at me before. He didn't care enough to get this angry at me before, but I was confused because I didn't know Scott while we were together.

I furrow my eyebrows and try to respond in a calm, even voice. "What're you talking about, Max? I didn't even know Scott until a week ago."

His cold expression doesn't change. "Yeah, not that you remember anyway. He let it slip that you guys met at a party and made out. Guess I'm not the only one who can't control their fuckin' alcohol."

SMACK. I slapped him as hard as I could, leaving a pink mark on his boney cheek.

He just chuckles and shakes his head. "That's what I thought. Get the hell outta my house now."

I don't move. I look at that bastard right in the eyes and dare him to look back. "You're a real asshole. And you wanna know why? I never got that drunk at a random party while I was with you."

He looks back at me, the firey ice in his eyes slowly melting. "I didn't even drink unless I was with you because the last time I got so smashed at a random party I was *raped*—" hot tears spilled out from my eyes, my voice shook, "and I didn't feel safe getting that drunk with anyone except you, Max. Because I trusted you. Because I *wanted* to have sex with you. Even though you fuckin' freaked out when I got pregnant and told me not to tell anyone and you forgot that my parents are fuckin' dead, and even though you don't know how they died exactly, that my father was an alcoholic and killed them both in that car crash. *I loved you despite all that you did.*"

His jaw slacks and eyes droop—guilt. Emotions build inside me, ones that I didn't realize I held in.

"I didn't ask for him to like me, Max!" My voice rises and I can still taste the cigarette smoke in my mouth, as if a fire is burning inside me. "But you know what? He's sure as hell nicer than you are— " *Bam*—I punch his chest. "You!"*—bam—* "FUCKING"*—bam—*"ASSHOLE!" *Bam bam bam*—tears break through me like hot lava, and he stands there, his body swinging like a punching bag. "I *loved* you! I would've done *anything* for you! But you know what, I'm not gonna end up like my mother. No. . . I can't. . ."

Bam, bam, bam. . . bam. . . my breathing gets heavy and panicky as my fists slow to a soft beat on his chest. He wraps his hands around my wrists and bends his head down to look at me.

I don't know what he wants and why he's acting this way now that he's broken my heart, but I feel darkness loom over me as he looks into my eyes, and that darkness in his eyes clear into a blue ocean.

"I'm so sorry," he whispers.

Max.

I kept trying to put the pieces together as Nura stood in front of me; the soft smell of roses and strawberries just barely covering up the cigarette smoke. She only ever smoked when it was really bad.

And it was really fuckin' bad.

"What the fuck, man!" Scott shouted, touching the blood dripping from his nose. I'd punched him pretty hard.

"GET OUT!" I ordered, pointing to the door.

I was about to push him out before he said—"Why are you mad? You guys weren't even together at the time! And you ended up meeting her at the bar again anyway!"

I stopped. "What're you talkin' 'bout? I met her for the first at the bar."

Scott chuckles and shakes his head. "No, you didn't. Last year. Labor Day weekend. We went to a party at UCSD. Nura was there."

A cold truth slapped my face.

Dark hair had flowed down her back and so many other people were dancing at Scott's party crowding around us, her, but I picked her out. I could pick her out from any crowd, and maybe it's because she still haunts me.

Because it wasn't the first time I'd seen her that way.

At the UCSD party almost a year earlier, a mysterious girl swayed her hips in curvy lines that matched the curves of her body, from foot to ankle, hip to waist, waist to smooth, round breasts filling her tight tank top, from her collarbone to her neck, her jaw to cheekbone—all natural curves that made her both sexual and beautiful, like an angel with broken wings, brought into darkness.

A flash of pink and yellow neon seemed to just sparkle on her golden skin in that darkness, and darkness that I might have brought her in. She smiled as she danced, and I drew closer to her—she smelled like roses and strawberries and cigarettes.

Once I realized it, all the tension in my body collapsed as I stood in front of Scott. My fists let loose. My chest sank to my feet.

He smirked and crossed his arms. He knew he'd gotten me.

"I don't—I don't remember that." I shook my head in denial.

He chuckled. "Well I'm not surprised. You were pretty fucked, man."

He was right, and it made me uneasy and tingly, like a ghost was creeping up behind me and there was no way for me to see it. I didn't like it. There was no way I. . . but . . .

At the bar, Tough Luck, a beautiful girl with dark hair flowing down her bare back smiled at me, her tight, black dress hugging every one of her curves:

"I'm Nura."

I leaned into her, whispering in her ear, and she smelled like roses and strawberries. Familiar. Like an angel with lashes for wings, fluttering over her golden eyes with darkness.

Roses and strawberries . . . and cigarettes.

What the hell have I done?

Chapter 29: Black Moon

It was a dark night
and the moon was gone
swallowed in darkness
It's not a new moon
because it's been here before.
It's empty. Cold in my eyes.
A black moon.

- Nura Hart

"I'm so sorry," he says again, still standing in the hallway outside his room. I don't want to move because his second apology strikes me so deep in my heart that I'm afraid of what he is sorry for—for all that he's done to me? For something he has done that I don't know about just yet? For what he is *going* to do?

A flash of that night comes back to me—the shadow looms over me and blocks all light in my world and speaks and—

No, it wasn't him.

It couldn't have been—there's no way I would've forgotten his face, those eyes, that voice. His voice.

"Max," I say through heavy sobs. Drowning—I can't see where is up or down. *Where is the safe place now?*

His lips tremble and fall and eyes drip out tears that I never thought was possible for him to shed, not for me anyway.

"I can't do this, Max. . . I think. I think you were right, before, you know. For breaking up with me in the first place. You don't need a girl, and I need a man." He presses his lips in a straight line at the last part; I knew it would hurt him, but not as much as he hurt me. Because at least I was telling him the truth.

My heart pangs with ache, but once I say that, a relief spreads over me. “Goodbye, Max,” and just as I whip around to walk out that door—

“I love you,” he whispers.

I freeze.

I turn right back around and slam my lips onto his and let my body take over and wash the now open wounds, even if it’s just a temporary fix. I don’t know why I still feel this way toward him—hypnotized. Maybe it’s because I’m drawn to the ocean and he’s the ocean and I’m the sand, and during a black moon night, we can’t separate. We will always be loving and destructive together, but the destruction feels worth it as he smooths his calloused fingers up my shirt and slips it off my body for the loving.

And then I’m back to that night and I don’t know why.

I pressed a hand against the sweaty skin of my belly and grinded against him, my head too fuzzy to care to wonder who it was. I smiled and shook my hair and gazed at the flicker of poison neon circles—the only source of light in the darkness.

Max?

I open my eyes and he's shirtless and we're in his room, like we always have been. The safe place. We've never had sex anywhere else. *Right*?

No. Stop thinking, Nura.

That's not hard to do when he kisses my neck and lays me on the bed, his body moving on top of mine. My black bra lays on the floor and I rip my shorts off my legs and suck in his air as our lips envelope each other.

Max.

It was hot and fuckin' sweet, her body. It always was. The sweetest strawberry melted in rose and soaked in her skin, every inch of her tan, smooth skin. And as I pressed my lips on her inner thighs, her body curled and she let out a moan.

I want to feel like this forever—kissed, loved, longed for—I want to suck in every nerve that tingles and explodes when he touches me. Everywhere. Anywhere. And I never want to *not* be touching him. Everywhere. Anywhere.

Always.

Max.

Golden. Her eyes had a golden glow in the light, and her brown hair weaved with gold hair fell around her face as she sat up.

I reached to kiss her, her face in my palms. And I slid one hand across her collarbone, her breast, her stomach, and underneath her last piece of clothing: seamless, black, wet.

Clouds of breath rise up my chest and escape through my lips as he takes off my underwear and presses his fingers in me and kisses my cheeks, my neck, my breasts. His hands and lips and tongue are the reasons why I'm able to forget my first time filled with stains of black blood.

Max.

I smiled and slid on top of her. "Shhh, it's okayyy," I whispered in her ear.

Her breathing became hard and excited. “Hmm, Max—” she said through one of those breaths.

There’s a bottle of Grey Goose on a shelf. And a flash of darkness, that darkness. Drinking the rest of that vodka to forget that night and . . oh god oh god—

Max.

I stripped the belt off my pants.

Zzziiip.

Another breath, but sharp, knife-like–

BAM.

“NO!” She pushed me off of her so quick and hard that I almost fell off the bed, pants unzipped and sliding off my legs.

What the fuck?

I stared at her, huddled at the end of the bed, her head between her knees.

She sobbed.

And I knew it was over.

Chapter 30: Red Eclipse

The sun betrayed me
Burned me
Red
And black
Scarred
Forever.

- *Nura Hart*

The shadow loomed over me.

"*Shhhhhhh*, it's okay." His whisper penetrated my ears, the cold poison paralyzing me. One hand fell onto my breasts, unwelcomed. Trailed under my skirt, unwelcomed.

Zzziiip.

I lay in that bed for what felt like forever. Bleeding. Sore. Broken.

But after what felt like too long in that darkness, seeing him over and over, I put on my clothes and stumbled out of the room.

And I bumped into a boy. A tall boy with blue eyes like the ocean and a voice like crackling velvet in the blur of my drunkenness.

"Whoa, you okay?" He said, catching me before I fell to the ground.

I shook my head and fell into his chest. "Yeah . . ." I looked up to see who I leaned on, and those eyes were so striking against the dark contrast of his dark that I was hypnotized from that very moment and I knew I would be doomed for as long as I looked into them: a clear ocean blue, the kind that lures you to swim even though the waves might drown you with their sudden turbulence.

And without thinking, I kissed him, his breathe tasting of alcohol and vanilla smoke that I wanted to swallow and keep for as long as I could.

"Hey! Max!" Someone shouted. The boy broke away from me.

"Sorry. Gotta go. But drink this." He handed me a water bottle seemingly out of nowhere.

I was left once again. Broken but fluttering at the same time; could such a dark experience be washed away so quickly?

I thought I'd be okay until I vomited chunks of food and cherry-colored liquid, contaminating my breath with acid and half-digested chips. I forced myself back into that dark room. A few white pills lay on the ground next to a bottle. I pick it up, and it's empty—OxyContin. I take one and look for something to chase it with. I knock over a bottle alcohol, partly filled. Grey Goose. I gulped down the rest of the vodka so I wouldn't remember this. Any of it.

And I dragged myself back on that violated bed.

I hoped to sleep and wake up from this nightmare.

I don't.

I'm huddled on the bed and Max stares at me, fear and blue ghosts clouded in his eyes.

I want to scream, but instead I hyperventilate, my chest huffing up and down so fast I think I'm dying.

He said we met at the bar, but then why do I remember seeing him before that? Am I going crazy? Or maybe we did meet and he doesn't remember—I wouldn't be surprised. But I knew he was there. I know that now.

"You know," I whisper, curled up in the corner of Max's bed.

He doesn't speak for a long time. Too long.

"Know what?" he croaks. But he knows exactly what I'm talking about.

"You were there that night."

And when I look him dead in the eyes, he just sits there on the bed, a safe distance from me. On his bed, we've slept, kissed, loved, broken, belittled and betrayed. This time he doesn't even bother to deny anything. And the love I had for him burns and crumples with hot ashes within me.

Tears carve down my skin like lava, but I do not let out a sound. I just stare. Because these are not tears of sadness, no, no more of that. These are tears of a girl who has finally shattered the glass mirage of the boy who is not the water that she needs to live.

"Nura. . ."

"*Don't,*" I snap.

I stand up and throw the grey blanket at him. The stupid blanket that I let him fuck me on. The pillows that our heads lay on. The sheets that he came on too late so the fucker got me pregnant. I want to scream and hit him and make him bleed like I had bled— make him hurt, even just a little—hurting him the way he's hurt me would take
much more than a few swipes to his deceivingly beautiful face.

"Nura! Wait!"

I whip my head around and fume, "YOU HAD THE NERVE TO ACCUSE ME OF CHEATING ON YOU WHEN IT WAS YOU ALL ALONG! YOU *RUINED* ME!" I can't breathe and I sound like I'm dying, choking, but I keep going, "And then you let your best friend kiss me, and you get angry, or at least pretend to, and for what? So you can pass me around like a fucking joint? Fuck you, Max. I hope you go to hell."

He grabs my wrist and the blackness threatens to flash back to my mind but I push against him—I'm not going to be a little victim anymore.

"Just let me explain!"

That really ticks me off. "What could there be to explain? You're a monster."

His grip on my wrist loosens. I flick his hand away and try to recover my lungs to even breaths from the panic and angry sobs, but there's only so much I can do. My cheeks are still boiling with tears, but I hope it looks like I've been burned so he can see what he's done.

"Nura, I'm so sorry," he says.

I laugh, hysterical. "Max, loving you has been harder than trying to breathe underwater, but not anymore. Because I'm done. And don't worry, I can't press charges anyway. Not enough evidence. But I'm done. *We're* done." I grab my things and slam the door behind me, all in one motion.

When I get back into my car, I do not collapse into sobs. I do not cry and feel bad for myself. I do not hate myself.

I just drive.

I drive and feel the heat of what I once thought was the sun, now eclipsed by the moon, and in the red outline betrayal burns in the sun's rays. What I thought was the sun and love was just darkness.

And it won't destroy me again.

Chapter 31: White Pills

Life's so fucked codeine ain't enough to numb this pain
– MAX.

I wanted to go after her, but I knew that she wouldn't listen to me. I took a swig of the Grey Goose vodka sitting on my shelf. Some liquid courage.

I grabbed my wallet and keys to head out, but when I swung the door open so hard it slammed against the wall, Scott stood at my doorstep with a sorry-ass look on his face.

"Hey man—"

"I don' have time right now, just leave." I shoved him out of my way.

"Hey man I'm sorry! Shit, if I knew you were gonna act like this—"

"Whatever." I unlocked my black BMW.

"Max—"

I hopped in my car, but before I could even turn on the engine and back out, not caring if I ran over the bastard, he hopped in the passenger seat.

"Get out."

"Nah, dude. You're fuckin' high and drunk—I can smell you from here."

"Whatever."

I press the gas and swing out of the gated neighborhood, not sure exactly where I was going, but knowing that I had to find Nura. Maybe her apartment?

"Dude, slow down," Scott said, holding onto the ledge of the car door.

"Why?" I asked.

"Cause you're gonna kill us!"

"Maybe you shouldn't have gotten in the car then."

"Shit imma need somethin' if I'm gonna die now." He took out a bottle of pills from his pocket, rattling a couple onto his palm.

I slammed the brake on a stoplight and white pills rained all over the car.

"The fuck man! That's a full bottle of Oxy right there!" Scott yelled.

My head snapped toward him as cars honk behind me. The light turned green.

It all crashed back to me.

I drove and pulled over to a gas station, leaving Scott in the car so I could call Nura. She didn't answer, but I left a voicemail to let her know the truth. She needed to know the truth.

It wasn't me.

Labor Day weekend. Scott had moved back to town and had some friends at UCSD to hook us up with some coke.

We both smoked a bunch before the party. I drank some Grey Goose. Scott was driving, so just smoked more.

When we took our last hits before headin' out to some parties, he was like, "Bet that I can get laid within the first two hours of bein' there?"

"Ha, sure man." I pat his shoulder and threw my car keys to him.

Only a half hour had passed into the party when I finished most of the bottle of Grey Goose and dropped it somewhere in the bedroom, where I brought some short blonde girl. I charmed her into giving me a blowjob in a bedroom—I was too drunk to really fuck her but it was enough for me to cum in her mouth.

I zipped up my pants, ready to leave the bedroom, but she grinned at me, her bright, devilish green eyes staring at me as she took out a small Ziploc bag from her shorts pocket. I smiled.

"Ahhh, bad girl."

We snorted the coke and left the bedroom together, but I ditched her to look for Scott.

Probably still tryin' to get laid, that kid.

I pushed into the crowd of drunk people and found him dancing with a girl; dark hair and curvy body dotted in bits of neon circles.

It was just so fuckin' crowded. I wanted to leave.

Sweaty bodies and red plastic cups merged together as I fought through arms to get to Scott. Finally, I got close enough to bump Scott on the shoulder. He turned around, still holding the girl by her waist.

"Hey! Let's hit the bars soon. I'm bored," I said. Scott nodded, his gold hair bobbing up and down—he was so high, this kid.

"Got it!"

And before I went to see if anyone had some weed, I saw her.

Dark hair in a tangled mess of curls and sweat and alcohol. She slipped down to the ground and laughed. People were too drunk to really notice. They just kept dancing, even Scott.

"Whoa," I said, bending down to her.

She parted her hair out of her face and smiled.

"Oops," she giggled.

My ears drew toward the sound. "You okay?"

"Ah ya, I fall all the time," she said. Before I could offer her a hand, Scott pulled her arms up from the ground and chuckled.

"Damn, Imma get her some water," Scott said, his eyes squinting and face stuck in a permanent, high grin.

I nodded and pat his shoulder. "Yea, let's get outta here soon. I'm gonna smoke a bowl first."

"Alrigh'." Scott held the girl and pulled her away from the ocean of limbs. I watched until they fell into a black cloak of the hallway.

I wondered what her name was, but it didn't matter at the time that much. I just wanted to get high. I wouldn't see her again anyway. Or I thought I wouldn't.

I don't know how much time had passed, but I do remember that blonde girl found me again and asked to dance. So I did until my forehead dripped sweat and my mouth thirsted for some fuckin' water.

I went to the kitchen and grabbed a water bottle in the fridge and I gulped the whole bottle down. I reached for my vape in my pocket—vanilla flavor—and looked around for Scott again, wanting to get the fuck outta there already.

I went to the hallway of rooms, thinkin' he might be in there with that chick. Before I could look though, a girl stumbled out of one room and pressed her body against the wall—I caught her before she could tumble to the ground.

"Whoa, you okay?" I said.

And it was her. The girl Scott had been dancing with—it was Nura. Soft tan skin. Large, brown eyes framed with thick, black lashes and dimmed sparkles. Even in her melting makeup and tangled hair, she was beautiful.

She shook her head and fell into my chest. "Yeah . . ." she moaned, then looked up at me and stared so deeply into my eyes I thought maybe she was a siren hypnotizing me with the water in her teary eyes, asking me to save her.

She kissed me.

I kissed her back, tasting roses and strawberry and cigarettes.

"Hey! Max!" Someone shouted. I turned around, craning my neck to see a hand wave in a crowd of people. Scott.

"Sorry. Gotta go. But drink this." I handed her the water bottle.

Then left without thinking about her again.

In the car, Scott chuckled as we walked outside to my car. "You know that girl I was dancing with? We were both so smashed. Damn, she's hot. She smelled like cigarettes, but fruity, too. Even tasted fruity," he boasted. I laughed and we slapped our hands together and half-hugged.

"So you fuck her?" I asked.

Scott hopped into the driver's seat, not looking one bit as smashed as I was. He grinned.

Nura didn't answer my call, and I didn't expect her too.

But I left a voicemail that explained everything. How I knew who it was. What happened. Everything. That I was sorry. God, I was sorry.

I walked back to the car and Scott was picking up the Oxys and putting them back in his bottle.

You stupid fuck.

I got back in my car and didn't even wait for him to get in, but he jumped in right before I stepped on the gas, skidding onto the road even faster than before.

"What the hell jus' happened? Dude, you're gonna kill us!" He shouted. But all I could hear was the damning truth from the bastard's lies. And her voice haunting me, asking me why I didn't save her.

"Was I really your first?"

"No," she whispered. "I don't really remember my first time."

"Do you know who it was?"

"No. It was too dark, and I was too drunk. A labor day weekend party."

"I didn't even drink unless I was with you because the last time I got so smashed at a random party I was raped*—"*

"Why did you wanna have sex? With me? . . ."

"Because. . . you don't take Oxy."

"You know that girl I was dancing with? We were both so smashed. Damn, she's hot. She smelled like cigarettes, but fruity, too. Even tasted fruity."

Son of a bitch.

"MAX LOOK OUT!" Scott screamed.

It ended in blackness.

Chapter 32: Stained Sheets

I killed the girl I love.

– Max. Haunted.

I fall onto my bed, grey sheets crumbled up. The alcohol still buzzes through me. I reach my hand out, tapping on empty spaces like my drums.

I turn my head to the space:

A lifeless puddle of sheets.

Except they're not grey sheets, they're white.

They're hers. I've been sitting next to Nura for a few hours, my hand on hers. Thinking about how this all happened. How I've hurt her.

Cold, lifeless. Lifeless.

Scott Jameson and Nura Hart were in critical condition, and I've been crying, for *her*.

For her soft, tan skin now shattered and black and purple and red from bruises and blood. Her eyes framed with curly, black lashes now stained with scratches from the shards of glass.

Her heart beeps on the monitor, steady and stable, for now, at least.

Scott's still in surgery, but to be honest, I don't care if he dies. Not anymore. In fact, I don't think I would care if I was in Nura's place because I deserve it just as much as Scott. All I've got is a headache banging across my skull, but that's probably from the alcohol.

Nura hit the passenger seat of my car because I was turning left at a yellow light and she kept going at a red light. I got lucky. I left that crash with barely a scratch—slight concussion and some cuts on my arms from the broken glass. And the crash was her fault, so the police didn't even look at me. I just took an Uber to the hospital.

Still, I shouldn't have been driving. *Even though you fuckin' freaked out when I got pregnant and told me not to tell anyone and you forgot that my parents are fuckin' dead, and even though you don't know how they died exactly, that my father was an alcoholic and killed them both in that car crash. I loved you despite all that you did.*

Her words haunt me. It all haunts me.

"Nura, I'm so sorry," I whisper for the millionth time, hoping she can hear me. Thinking that she probably can't.

God, what the fuck have I done?

"Max."

I look up and V stomps in the hospital room, eyes puffy and red. Brows knit together. Jaw clenched.

I let go of Nura's hand. V shakes her head at me. Makeup drips from her eyes as she leans toward me and sniffs.

She slaps me.

"You're a fucking shithead."

I gulp and bend my head down.

"Yeah."

She drags a chair to the other side of Nura's bed and sits down.

"Nura called me and told me what happened."

I don't say anything. I look at Nura—she's still asleep, but maybe she's hearing everything that we're saying. Or maybe she's screaming in pain.

"She said it was Scott. He raped her, and she thought it was you, but she got your voicemail and remembered. She was driving back to see you."

I open my mouth to say something, anything, but nothing comes out.

"Even though she ran the red light, I blame you."

"Me too." Even though I wasn't the guy who raped her, I was the guy that left her. Over and over again. And hurt her. And was a jackass who only cared about getting high and drunk. In fact, I wish I was high right now.

Even though I wasn't the one that took her into that room, that took her, I could have helped her. I could have been a better guy and made sure Scott was just getting her water.

I hold her hand again and squeeze it this time, trying to get her warm again. "You don't have to forgive me this time, Nura," I whisper, burying my head in the sheets, now stained with my pathetic tears that're probably filled with vodka.

I even fuckin' pray. I pray to God that she can just leave this hospital in one piece and be happy and I promise to leave her life forever if that's what it takes. God, I probably won't change, but she should live because she's a good person.

That's when I feel it.

Her fingers twitch and flutter against mine.

Angels gave her back her light. Nura Hart. Light.

Chapter 33: Bitter Butterscotch

Sun inside a skull
by the base of his neck
sun's flames
peek out
from an empty skull

- *Nura Hart*

A pool of bodies and red solo cups swirl around Nura Hart in a pleasant, watery haze. She stumbles her way to the dance floor. The music thumps in the claustrophobic nightmare of darkness and poison neon circles of light. She slithers through the crowd and starts to move her hips 'round and 'round until a guy draws toward her and dances behind her.

She presses his hand against the sweaty skin of her belly and grinds against him, not knowing who it was and not seeming to care. She grins and grips her hair with her hands and slides her body down against the stranger—she's high and happy and hazy.

"*OOOOH*!" People shout from the kitchen. Max Sommer won the game of beer pong. Satisfied, he leaves the kitchen and dives into an ocean of limbs floating and swinging on the dance floor as a small blonde girl clings to his side. They disappear into a bedroom.

Nura Hart dances with the guy and turns, her eyes closed, and swallows his tongue and lips until her lips are swollen. The guy breaks apart from her and turns her around, slamming the back of her against him.

Max and the girl come out from the bedroom. He looks for his friend back in the dance crowd. Nura falls onto the ground and laughs.

“Whoa,” Max says, bending down to her.

“Oops,” she giggles.

“You okay?” he asks.

“Ah ya, I fall all the time,” she says, and the guy she was dancing with pulls her up and chuckles.

“Damn, Imma get her some water,” he says.

“Yea, let’s get outta here soon. I’m gonna smoke a bowl first,” Max says to his friend.

“Alrigh’.” The guy holds the girl.

“Whaterereya, wherya gonin’?” Nura asks the guy as he pulls her away from the crowd.

Max watches them disappear in a black hallway.

“Don’ worry—I’ll take care you ya,” the guy tells Nura. His arms, a cascade of lanky muscles, drags her forward. He takes her inside a bedroom, pitch black with the exception of a single strand of moonlight from the window.

Click.

He locks the door and pushes her forward, tossing her onto the bed. She tries to speak, the force briefly allowing her to wake. "Wa—wha—wa—"

"*Shhhhhh.*" He presses his finger against her lips. She flicks it away and her whole body flips to the side. She shakes her head, her hair whipping in her face.

"No, I—Ineedagohome," she whines and tries to sit up. But before she can lift herself off the bed, he smacks her back down and weighs his body—sweaty and heavy—against hers.

"*Shhhhh.*" His hand strokes her hair. Soft, silent.

Nura shivers and cries.

"St—st—don't. *Stop—*" She rolls over, crawling toward the edge of the bed so that maybe the fall will allow her enough time and strength to run.

"Hey, don't fall there." He grabs her and pins her down, his hands chain-tight around her wrists. A bottle of OxyContin falls from his pocket, next to a partly filled bottle of Grey Goose vodka.

"He—l—*help,"* she croaks.

"*Shhhhhhh*, it's okay." A bit of moonlight cuts through the cracks of the curtains—a flick of sun-blonde hair and white grin glows in the light. His eyes penetrate her—deep gold, like butterscotch rotting black.

Ziiippppp.

"Shhhhhh."

Scott Jameson shoves himself inside Nura Hart.

He smiles.

Chapter 34: Vanilla Smoke

Puffs of sweet, steamy clouds—
inhale—
air floods my lungs
scent seizes my mind—
vanilla smoke
trapped in my closed mouth
begging to be let go
so I open my lips
And we're free

- *Nura Hart*

As I drove on the road along the beach, windows down, salty, sunset air drying my tears, my phone rang.

Da da da da dun da da da, da da da da da dun da da

Darling you got to let me know

Da da da da da dun da da

Should I stay or should I go

da da da da da dun da da

If you say that you are mine

I'll be here 'til the end of time

So you got to let me know

Should I stay or should I go?

A few minutes passed, and my phone beeped again. A voicemail.

My curiosity burned because I wanted to know what he had to say but I didn't want him to know that I wanted to hear his "explanation." He wouldn't know if I listened to the voicemail though. *If it's bullshit, I'll just delete it.*

So I clicked on the voicemail.

"Nura please let me explain. It was Scott. Yes, I was there that night. But I didn't know until now that he did it. That he hurt you. He was telling me about that night earlier and something didn't add up but he slipped, Nura, he had Oxys and spilled them all over the car and he mentioned that you smoke cigarettes that night that—that night. He told me he was with a girl. It was you. I saw you. And you smelled like cigarettes." A pause. He choked up and sniffed. "I'm so sorry Nura. I'm so sorry."

I made an immediate U-turn. I had to see him and know if it was true. I wanted him to look me in the eyes and tell me that was the truth.

But the dark pits of my mind and stomach, sick and disgusted, told me it was.

Scott Jameson raped me.

I open my eyes.

Max.

"I'm so sorry," I say and slowly inch my hand toward her shoulder.

She doesn't stop me. Of course she wouldn't, she loves me too much and I know that and I always knew that and I was an idiot I *am* fucking idiot.

I'm too selfish to let her go. But guilt beats me up, saying that I have to. That was God's fucking condition.

Very funny, you bastard.

His fingers touch my cheek and his palm puddles on my skin. Maybe I'm in heaven, but the small cuts on his face and the sharp angles of his sullen cheeks tell me that this could not be heaven.

Because this version of him would not be in my heaven. It would be the version that I thought was there but never was and probably never could.

Still, I pretend. At least for a little while.

Max.

She closes her eyes and presses her face against my hand, her tickling my fingers. I have to let her go.

"Nura," V whispers, putting a hand on my shoulder. My lips crack into a smile. I wince, my whole body achy, but I'm alive and my best friend is here. Max is here.

"V." I reach my hand out, shaking.

V sobs. "Don't scare me like that again you bitch." I laugh and my bones feel like they're cracking, but I just want to smile.

"I'm sorry," I cry.

She hugs me but doesn't squeeze—she knows I'm hurting. And she knows me, so she nods over at Max—*do you want to talk to him?*

I nod at her. She gets up from her chair and leaves the room.

Max clears his throat and smiles at me. "Hey. How you feelin'?"

"Like I got in a car crash," I joke. He shakes his head.

"I'm sorry, Nura."

"I know you are, Max." My voice cracks. The tears that fall down my face sting my skin, but I let them fall because I know what happens next.

And it hurts.

He holds my hand and we're quiet for a moment, enjoying the only real, intimate silence that we've ever had.

. . .

. . .

. . .

His smoky voice seeps through it. "I never told you. . . Nura. . ."

"I told me what?"

"I love you."

My lips curve up and down in one motion. "You have."

"I know, but—"

"It's okay, Max. I forgive you." I squeeze his hand and hold it to my lips for only a breath because I know I have to let go of it eventually. Of him.

"You don't have to," he says. His eyes as sincere as I thought they could be.

I place his hand back on the edge of my bed. "I know."

And even though the world seems as if it will be less sweet, less bright without being able to love him, something hopeful comforts me: that maybe, just maybe, we'll have both changed for the better after all of this.

We may have been meant to be together, but not forever. Just for a moment.

And so when I say to him, “We can let go now,” he seems to understand.

He kisses my forehead, stands up, then simply touches my lips with his so as not to hurt me, but I press my hand on the back of his neck so he’ll kiss me harder because *screw* the pain. It’s only temporary.

And as I open my eyes, his just blinks from mine, I see the ocean, where I’ll always belong, where my soul will belong forever. But I know that can share that world with someone else. Water flows through my body and heart. I just won’t swim with him anymore.

I let go of the vanilla smoke.

Acknowledgements

First of all, thank you, reader, for your time. I appreciate the time you've taken to specifically read the first book that I've actually been brave enough to put out there, and this is something I am proud of. I hope that this story has brought something of value to you.

Of course, I could not have done it without the help of my friends and family, especially Kim, my professor and guardian, who has been a huge support throughout my college career and writing. You have pushed me to grow as a writer and a person, which, I think, go hand-in-hand.

Thank you to my many families who have supported me throughout my life in, thank you to the life-long friends I have made and read over drafts of this story over and over.

And, I must mention my fellow writer-—Josey.

Y'all are awesome.

95997472R00178

Made in the USA
San Bernardino, CA
17 November 2018